the
bliss house

the
bliss
house

JIM BARTLEY

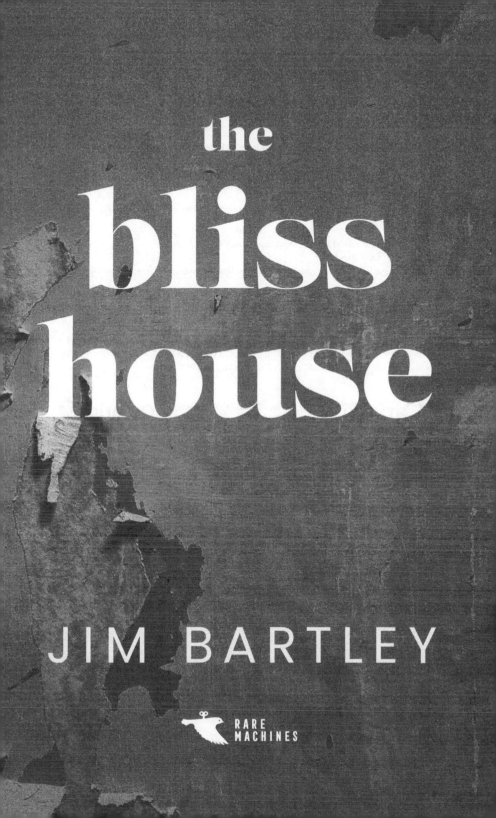

RARE
MACHINES

Publisher: Kwame Scott Fraser | Acquiring editor: Russell Smith
Cover designer: Laura Boyle
Cover image: Fan: unsplash.com/Rajat Sarki; wallpaper: shutterstock.com/Russell Watkins

Library and Archives Canada Cataloguing in Publication

Title: The bliss house / Jim Bartley.
Names: Bartley, Jim, 1952- author.
Identifiers: Canadiana (print) 20220464456 | Canadiana (ebook) 20220466238 | ISBN 9781459751460 (softcover) | ISBN 9781459751477 (PDF) | ISBN 9781459751484 (EPUB)
Classification: LCC PS8553.A777 B55 2023 | DDC C813/.54—dc23

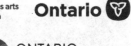

We acknowledge the support of the Canada Council for the Arts and the Ontario Arts Council for our publishing program. We also acknowledge the financial support of the Government of Ontario, through the Ontario Book Publishing Tax Credit and Ontario Creates, and the Government of Canada.

Care has been taken to trace the ownership of copyright material used in this book. The author and the publisher welcome any information enabling them to rectify any references or credits in subsequent editions.

The publisher is not responsible for websites or their content unless they are owned by the publisher.

Printed and bound in Canada.

Rare Machines, an imprint of Dundurn Press
1382 Queen Street East
Toronto, Ontario, Canada M4L 1C9
dundurn.com, @dundurnpress 𝕐 f ◎

the
burning

1

August 1963

CAM BLISS SHARES A BEDROOM with Dorie on the second floor. Dorie needs someone to sleep with her or she spooks. The view is easterly. It's summer and the days begin with sunlight beaming straight across the cornfields from the horizon. The first rays hit the underside of the eaves, like the sun is actually lower than the house. If Cam wakes up at the right time, he sees this orange light on the flaking white paint. He thinks it has to be impossible. But there it is. He remembers it from as far back as anything. Then the sun comes onto the rose wallpaper above the bed, making the pink pinker. If Dorie doesn't wake up ahead of him and start her jabbering, he can lie quiet, watching the light and shadow move across the flowers.

Cam is seventeen now. He went to a special school in Hanover until he was fifteen. The school was in somebody's house. Cam was more normal than the other kids and he always knew that. He talked funny and misbehaved and got bad grades, so they put him there. Then they let him try the regular high school, but that was only for a year because Gran died, and Gramp took him out to help at home. He can read. That's one good thing they taught him. Since he got out, he's read a lot of books from the Walkerton Public Library.

Dorie is five and she's never been to school yet. She came when she was just a baby almost. Gran and Gramp took her from some relatives in Hamilton because they couldn't have a kid with them.

Since January, Gramp has been in the cold room, a tin-roofed lean-to off the back of the old kitchen. When they found Gramp stiff on the sofa the morning after New Year's, Cam phoned his cousin Wes Cody right away. He came and he said they had to find Gramp's will. They looked all through the house and the pumphouse, too, where Gramp sometimes slept off his binges. They even went through Gran's old things and there was nothing. A whole day searching and they found some hid whisky bottles but that was it. Wes put Gramp out in the cold room and that's where he's stayed, wrapped up tight in heavy plastic and covered with a tarp held down with bricks.

Wes is older, maybe ten years older than Cam. He had a part-time job in Hamilton, but with Gramp gone, he started staying most days at the farm again. Then one day he just called up his boss and quit. Wes is related to Dorie but he's not her father. She's a Price and Wes is a Cody. According to Wes, Dorie's mother was a drug addict. She went to Toronto and never came back. The Codys and Prices aren't Bliss family — they're on Gran's side. Wes was always around and worked on the farm from the time Cam was little.

After Gramp died, they hardly ever went in the cold room. They just didn't talk about what was in there. In the spring Wes sealed the gaps around the inside door with tape, but that didn't really solve the problem. What solved it was Cam's own idea: a small electric fan. He installed it in the cold room window and left it permanently on, to blow out the stink. He planned how to do it for most of a sleepless night and he spent a whole day rigging it and it worked. Wes said it would do fine. He just put some caulking around the gaps. The decay smell gets back into the house during a strong north wind or a power outage, but they live with that.

Gran died first. She was sick for a few months and then she was gone. Gramp tried to cook on their big Happy Thoughts wood stove that's as old as the house, but his cooking was terrible. Cam took over and did better, but not like Gran. He used the electric Moffat. Even Gran used the Moffat in summer, but she talked about the expense. Now Cam is in charge of supper. Wes is here all the time. He does the shopping for food and some beer just for himself. Things have changed. But it's working out good. Gramp made their life hell.

There's money in the bank in Wingham. The land-lease arrangement means neighbours pay them to farm their land, and it means steady income if the crops grow all right, and mostly they do. They still get Gramp's government pension, too. They don't have to pay for anything, really, except for food and electricity. Water and firewood come with the land, same as forever.

Once a month Wes drives to the bank and takes out money. It was all arranged by Gran, when Gramp started drinking worse and wouldn't even leave the house. Gran knew that she was getting sick, too. Wes and Cam went to the bank with her and Wes signed some papers. Gran explained to Cam there's a savings account and chequing account and Wes would take care of the money things if anything happened to her or Gramp. Now Wes is completely in charge. They never say anything to anyone about Gramp dying. Wes says the farm could be lost, the house, the land, and everything, because there's no will.

Gramp got a TV antenna put up on the roof, so the television gets two channels that are good enough to watch. Dorie watches a lot. Wes makes her eat meals at the table, but he lets her leave early if *The Munsters* is coming on. Cam likes *Bonanza* and *Dragnet* and *Highway Patrol.*

Dorie eats a sandwich (usually peanut butter) and milk and sometimes Cheezies for lunch. For breakfast it's Cheerios or Sugar Pops, but Cam eats mostly fried eggs and toast. Cam likes a lot of different things and knows how to make them: spaghetti with meat sauce, beans with sliced wieners, peas with Minute Rice and chicken gravy, fish sticks with tartar sauce. He fries Spam and makes sandwiches with Cheez Whiz and bread-and-butter pickles. One thing that Cam misses is Gran's apple pies and apple butter. Apples didn't cost anything. They had more than they could use. Gran made delicious pies. The pies they get from the supermarket are just sweet and gloppy with no spice.

Gramp had a brother they used to see at Christmas, Uncle Earl, but that stopped because Gramp fought with him every time. Cam doesn't have parents anymore. They went away a long time ago. Gran said his mother sent some letters when he was a baby. Cam found the letters in a drawer after Gramp died and he read them. Basically, his father, Gramp's son, was no good. He drank and got in fights all the time, then he took off out West somewhere and disappeared. His mother had other problems, mental ones. The fact was, Gramp drank all the time too, but he never went away anywhere. He stayed home and made their life miserable.

Gramp got something that made him sick in his stomach. He couldn't eat almost anything. He ate oatmeal mostly, every meal. Cam boiled the water and stirred the oats and put it always in the same bowl for him, with a little sugar, no milk, and Gramp usually ate half or less. It went on for a long time. He wouldn't go to the doctor. He got thin. He started sleeping on the daybed in the old kitchen. It's the warmest room, and the coolest in summer if they don't use the wood stove.

The bathroom's upstairs, and that was a problem for Gramp at the end. Cam thought that maybe the bathroom problem was why Gramp gave up and died. Why else would he stop eating and then stop even drinking anything except booze? Wes came home from shopping a couple times without Gramp's whisky, but that just turned Gramp into a wild man. So Wes said, "Let the bugger kill himself if he wants."

There were a few months when Cam and Wes had to help Gramp upstairs to use the toilet. Then he couldn't. He used an old chair without the seat. He told Cam how to make it like a toilet and he used a bucket under the chair and Cam took it upstairs to dump it in the real toilet. The shit was black. Like tar. It smelled horrible, worse than normal shit. His pee stank and was dark brown. It was like Gramp's insides were rotting and coming out, and Cam and Wes had to carry his rotten insides up the stairs, more times a day than they could count.

Cam wasn't sad when Gramp died. Just relieved. Sometimes, later, at night he woke up and cried. Doric cried right away and then she was done. Cam's cries were not about being sad, not really. They seemed more about old memories that came back, none of them good.

But all of that is finished now. With just Wes around, things are better. All the crops are managed by the Johnstone family. The old tractor and harvester are rusting behind the barn, and the old Dodge truck. No one comes to the house anymore.

"They were never much for mixing" is what people say about the Bliss family. Outside of the kids and teachers Cam knew at school, he knows only faces, like at the public library, and the bank in Wingham. The doctor and dentist are in Walkerton, and then the clinic in Hanover where Gramp used to go to a doctor for his stomach, until he stopped.

Gramp had a temper. No one knew the real story about Gramp — only the family. He had rage fits. They happened because he drank. They were worse if Gran or anyone mentioned the drinking. Cam still has marks on his back and his behind from

Gramp's belt. Gramp didn't care if the buckle was at the wrong end, or maybe he wanted it that way. He went crazy mad and his face got red and he ranted about nothing, maybe just a spilled glass of juice or something, or that someone touched his tools, or he couldn't find something and blamed everyone. He broke Gran's teeth once and she told the dentist she fell against the stove. Gramp never hit Dorie. The worst she got was a few whacks on the bum from Gran. Gran had an old Ping-Pong paddle for that. Cam used to get it too, before. It was almost fun compared with what Gramp did.

Wes was always good to Cam. After the beatings, with Gramp usually passed out, Wes and Cam sometimes went to the hayloft. Wes sat with him while he lay down in the hay on his stomach because his backside was burning. The smell of the hay helped. Wes said, "I'll kill that bastard someday." But he never did. He tried to stop Gramp sometimes. But you couldn't stop Gramp. One time he swung a shovel at Wes and the blade sliced his arm open. The blood was squirting. Wes nearly called the police but Gran grabbed the phone away from him and started screaming at him, too.

Then, after Gran died, Gramp drank himself sick. Wes said the old bugger deserved to die and why should they bother. Cam thought he was right. The only one Gramp was ever nice to was Dorie. The one time anyone saw Gramp smile was when Dorie was doing a funny dance or something.

Cam can see they are not like any of the families on television. The only actual farm family is *The Real McCoys* with Walter Brennan. He's the grandpa but he is so much not like Gramp it's a joke, and anyway it's not anything like Bruce County. *Bonanza* doesn't count either, because they're cowboys.

On television, some of the boys have girlfriends and drive sporty cars and live in city houses. None of them sleep in a room with their little girl cousin. Sometimes they kiss their girlfriends.

Before they had a TV, Cam didn't know much about kissing or any of that. He doesn't like the kissing idea at all. Why do people do it?

2

WES STILL HATES GRAMP WHEN he thinks of him out there with the worms crawling — must be on the way to compost by now. Best to just leave him there, keep the fan going and blowing out the poison gas until he's rotted down to human fertilizer. Nobody's missed him. People knew he drank so they'll just write it off to that and forget him. Everyone around here wrote off the Bliss family years ago.

It's good the booze killed the bugger because Wes nearly did it himself a few times. He should've smashed Gramp's head that day with the same shovel that took a chunk out of his arm. He could've called it self-defence. Anyway, it's all over. Never again does he have to see Gramp whipping Cam or passed out on the floor with the whisky fumes coming off him.

Gramp left Dorie alone, never touched her at all. Dorie was the only one Gramp ever said a good word to. Wes knows Cam never deserved the beatings, not for anything he ever did. Cam is smarter than anyone thinks. The school he went to was a joke and he's better off now. The fact is they're all better off now than they've been in living memory.

If the old man had made a proper will, who knows who he'd have left the farm to. Cam would maybe be set, but you can't know that. So this is the situation. Gramp left no one to manage the place and Gran put Wes in charge of banking for the kids, so he's it now. The whole place is his responsibility. He thinks maybe he should report Gramp missing. Someday, but not yet. He has to work that out but there's no rush.

He doesn't shop in the stores anywhere local. He gets their food at the new Dominion Store in Goderich, and any hardware or similar stuff there, too — far enough away so that no one will look at him and say, "You're Wes, aren't you, up the Bliss place? How the folks doing these days?" They might say it in Walkerton or Wingham, but he knows it's only so he'll say everything's hunky-dory on the farm, so then they can think what a liar he is and what screw-ups the Blisses are, as if it's their friggin' business. The only stop in Wingham is the bank, and they don't ask him anything most times. The younger tellers don't know or care, anyway. If Cam's in with him, the older ones look at him like, "Oh that's the Bliss boy, the slow one." But he's sharper than they are.

If the kids get a toothache or sick or whatever, Wes thinks he'll just take them to Goderich instead of their old doctor. There's a clinic at the regional hospital. At home they've stopped answering the phone pretty much. The old man never answered unless it was expected and that's the way they still have it. There's no one to call them except some church charity wanting donations or just people being nosy, like the McKieran woman next door. There's the land lease with the Johnstone brothers and Wes will have to deal with that somehow when it comes up. But Wes just pays the phone bill and electricity and there's nothing else regular. The phone hardly rings.

Wes used to tell Cam that Gramp should have a forked tail. The man was Satan incarnate the last few years. When his face got boiling red in a rage, he even looked the part. Wes believes he had some sort of mind sickness. Now with Satan dead, the months since then don't feel real. It's like the yelling and crying are still in the walls, along with the crack of the leather belt.

Wes feels ashamed that he only stood by when Gramp got on a tear and beat Cam. He couldn't watch. He just listened out on the porch or pacing around the yard and he tore himself up for being such a coward. He stood up to Gramp just a few times and backed down every time, too. He pretty much gave up after the shovel, and then the time Gramp knocked him down with a few blows that left blood pouring from his mouth and his head ringing. Wes is still half-deaf in one ear. The man had fists like hammers.

But there was no one, no one else to watch out for Cam. Gramp knew how far he could go. He never left a mark on Cam's face. That might have pushed Wes to do something. His own father used a belt on him, so it seemed — well, not right exactly, never right, but a regular thing. He couldn't stop it. That shame is still in the house with Wes.

Now they are just starting to believe that nothing bad can happen. The ghosts are still around but they can't do any harm. Dorie said it one time when she found a booze bottle in behind the wood bin. There was about an inch of whisky left in it. She said what Gran said, "Devil water," and Cam said, "It's just no-good old whisky now."

Wes took the bottle and he went out the door. He walked to the barn with Cam and Dorie tagging behind him. He went round the back of the barn to the dry well and kicked the wood cover off it and he held the bottle over the hole. He said, "This bottle's going to hell." He dropped it into the well and after a little gap, there was a tinkling sound. They stared down the hole. Back in the house, they had ice cream.

Wes is not like a father or brother to Cam. It's something different. Wes just turned twenty-eight but he's never had a kid — never got married, either. He has a half-sister down in Brantford but he hasn't seen her for a few years now. She never came to the farm, anyway. Dorie is sometimes a handful, but Wes accepts that he's her guardian now. This job, taking care of the place and Cam and Dorie, just dropped into his lap. He could see what was coming and he thought about the part he would have. The old man was going to die and it was going to happen right here in the house. One day he just wouldn't wake up. And that's exactly what happened, only a lot messier.

A few weeks after Wes put the body in the cold room, he quit his rented basement in Hamilton. He was working only at a filling station by then and he quit that, too. No more work for him at Stelco since a new contract pushed the part-timers out. If they thought he was disposable, then screw them. He lives free now. He can sit on the porch with a beer and look at the fields and the sky and someone else driving a tractor back and forth to keep the money coming. He deserves it after all the bullshit and abuse. Dorie and Cam are his family. That's how it turned out, like it was meant that way. He wouldn't want any other life. Not without Cam, anyway.

Cam sits with him on the porch and reads. He reads quite a bit, books from the Walkerton Library. Wes takes him in and hops over to the diner in Mildmay for a bite, and he sometimes comes back with a hamburger for Cam. He took Cam up today to return some books and before Cam got out of the car he said he'd get a book for Wes, if he wanted. Wes hasn't read a book since he failed grade eleven and his dad got him a grunt job at the foundry. So he told Cam thanks, but no. Cam looked at him like he wanted to say more but he got out of the car and crossed the street to the library. He went up the steps and inside and it made Wes remember the time he was in there on a school outing, before his dad got the Hamilton job and moved them away. He remembered the quiet, and the book smell.

When Wes picked up Cam after lunch, he had three more books. They came in the house and Cam put them on the wicker table on the porch and he said Wes was free to read any of them. Now Cam is in the kitchen making up some supper and Wes is on the porch looking at a book by Ray Bradbury. Cam's real fond of this Bradbury fellow. Wes sets the book aside. The sun is blazing bright into the cornstalks to the east and Wes can see straight across the field to the neighbours' barn and the back of their house.

Dorie is sitting in the dry dirt under the maples, pushing her naked Barbie doll around in a toy pickup truck. Dorie is naked as the doll except for her red plastic sandals and Wes is thinking she should have some pants on at least, only because the McKieran woman telephoned again saying she didn't like her boys seeing that. Wes had to think, *Seeing what? Have they got binoculars?* The McKierans are only there since three or four years ago. They don't run the farm operation, just rent the house. The two boys do some field work for the Johnstones. Wes stares at the house and imagines he can see her now, looking out the back window.

"Dorie, go put some clothes on."

Dorie looks at him like he's not making any sense and goes right back to her Barbie world. The doll's hair is the same dirty tangle as Dorie's. He stares at the McKieran house and finishes the last of his Black Horse Ale. One more with his supper and that'll be it. Cam isn't legal to drink and never wants it, anyway. As long as Wes is here, hard liquor will never get back into the house.

Dorie makes her Barbie sing and dance around the pickup truck: "I love to poo, I really do …" Then she throws Barbie down. "Noooo!" She rubs Barbie in the dirt and runs her over with the truck.

Wes goes into the house.

Cam has made a pot of beans with chopped wieners and Heinz 57, and some sliced-up tomato and cucumber on a plate. They grow their own, and squash and potatoes too. They had runner beans and cauliflower and more but not so much since Gran died. Wes calls Dorie in and fills a bowl from a fresh bag of Cheezies. He makes himself and Cam a couple tomato sandwiches with Miracle Whip. The bread is soft and fresh from the supermarket that morning.

Wes makes Dorie get some pants on and then hold out her hands so he can wipe them with the dishrag. He's being like Gran when he does this, but he wonders why he bothers. Gran also said everyone's got to eat a peck of dirt before they die. Dorie must be up to the full peck by now.

"I looked at that Bradbury book, Cam."

"You read any yet?"

"I think I will later."

The meal goes quick and mostly quiet except for Dorie gabbing away about nothing they need to listen to. She won't eat cucumber or tomato but she loves beans and 57 and bread and butter. They all dip into the Cheezies. Wes has a beer and Dorie and Cam drink milk, sometimes chocolate for Dorie. That's dinner. Maybe some ice cream after, on the porch. Now with the old guy dead, they can buy it anytime.

3

IF EVERYTHING WAS CHEEZIES, SHE could eat them all day. Everything. The walls, the chairs, the sofa, not the stove because it would burn up, but everything else except people. She could take a Cheezie and every time a new Cheezie would appear in the same place like magic, so they would never run out. And the fridge would always be full of chocolate and regular milk, and ice cream in the freezer. The outdoor things can't be Cheezies because of rain and snow and there wouldn't be any proper trees or fields full of corn.

Cam and Wes are upstairs right now. She knows they play a game in Wes's room. Kyle McKieran played that kind of game with her once, in their barn, and his mother came and got real mad. But there's no one here to get mad at Cam and Wes. Now there's never anything like the yelling and whipping Gramp did on Cam. All of that is over. Except Gramp's out there in the cold room, but Wes says he's rotten now. Wes says they could grind him up and use him to fertilize vegetables, but it would probably kill them.

She loves Cheezies. She really really loves them. Cam says she can't eat them at breakfast time. Starting with lunch is okay. Cam makes her take One-A-Days. He saw them on TV and said she needs them because she never eats her vegetables. She hates vegetables, except peas with rice and gravy. She hates tomatoes and string beans, and asparagus makes her want to throw up. They all love corn on the cob and eat tons of it at picking time unless it's feed corn for cows. Corn always comes out the same in her poo.

Dorie is not her real name. She's Dorothy, but no one ever says that. Cam got her a library card that says Dorothy Price right on it. She's a Price. She never went to school yet so she can't read much, but Cam gets her picture books. After Gran died, Cam taught her reading from a book about a cat, but it's hard to remember all the words.

She thinks television is better than books because it's not work. You just watch. Everything happens like the whole world is there inside the TV, except the Munsters are not real people. On the news it's real people, like the tornado in Listowel that killed people in their house and broke cars and trees and threw cows up in the air like they were toys. That was real but the Munsters are fake. No family is like them. "Munster" means "monster," but they don't hurt anyone.

Now Dorie is outside under the maple tree with her Barbie. Cam makes her play out of the sun so that means under the trees or alongside the barn or in the barn. Right now she's digging a hole with an old kitchen spoon. Under the top dust, the dirt is hard and the spoon keeps bending. She's going to bury Barbie up to her neck and leave her there because she has been very bad, but the spoon is useless.

Then she thinks of the pump shed with all the tools and the digging thing like a big spoon, a spoon for the garden. She gets up and goes along past the rose bushes. Gran used to cut the roses for inside the house. She goes up toward the pump shed and she sees Wes is there with a wheelbarrow. When she gets closer, there is an awful smell. Wes tells her it's groundhogs. She can see them

in the wheelbarrow, fat and stiff with their legs sticking up. Wes
puts traps out beside their holes.

"Guess I should've picked them up before the rot set in.
Pee-yew."

Wes holds his nose and Dorie says, "Pee-yew," and holds hers,
too.

"Where you taking them, Wes?"

"We're gonna have them for supper tonight. Would you like to
skin 'em for me?"

Dorie just goes into the shed. Wes thinks he's funny. When
she sees the thing she wants, she knows the word. "Trowel." But
there's two of them. She takes the one with the red handle. When
she comes out, Wes is already on the path to the trash pit with the
dead groundhogs. She goes back to dig the hole for Barbie. She
wonders if people could really eat groundhogs.

The trowel works. She makes Barbie sit in the hole with her
arms straight up and buries her right up to her neck. Her head
looks so funny sticking up out of the ground, and her arms like
she's screaming, *Ahhhh! Pull me out!* Dorie has to do something
else to make it funnier. She goes back to the pump shed and fills
a watering can and comes back and waters Barbie. She sits cross-
legged for a long time, playing with the mud and putting it all over
Barbie's head until it's just a mud ball on a skinny neck.

4

CAM WONDERS ABOUT THE BODY. The smell is still there but not nearly as bad. When he goes out past the exhaust fan now, it's more like a natural rot, like the decay you smell in the woods or around swampy land. Gramp doesn't smell like death anymore, the kind of stink that sticks to everything and makes you want to get somewhere else fast before you puke.

He wants to ask Wes if there's a plan. Someone could come to the house. Cam is thinking they should bury Gramp. Roll him up in that big tarp and truck him down to the bottom of the north field where it's too soggy for crops and no one ever goes. But that would be too close. If anyone wants to come looking for him, they'll start right here on the farm. It's a complicated situation, just like on the murder shows on TV. Except nobody murdered Gramp.

He wanted to kill Gramp. He nearly did. They had to fix the lightning rod on the south peak of the barn because it got hit. Gramp made him help. They had to get up there and put a new glass on it.

Gramp got two ladders and they put one up to the roof and hauled the other one up with rope and they slid it up along the shingles to the peak. Cam got yelled at for chipping the shingles. Gramp made him climb the second ladder to the top to put the glass ball on. He did it okay but he was sweating and dizzy from the sun. Gramp was down at the top of the first ladder, jawing at him to make sure he got it right, and when Cam backed down from the peak he had a thought he'd just knock Gramp right off the ladder with one kick of his foot, like he'd slipped.

He didn't do it. Obviously. It would have been perfect. The perfect murder. But knowing Gramp he would've survived and Cam would get sent to jail for homicide. Or Grampicide. Attempted, anyway.

He's out picking corn for lunch. If it's possible to eat too much corn and butter, they probably got to that stage ages ago. The years they grow nothing but soybeans or rapeseed, there's no food worth picking. Technically they are stealing from the lessees, but the lessees are the Johnstone brothers a few miles over and nobody thinks about someone stealing for food off their own land, leased or not. But Cam knows they don't own the crop, just the field. So technically it's stealing. Just like technically they are stealing Gramp's pension money. That doesn't mean it's wrong.

Cam believes it even would've been right to kill Gramp. He was like an Adolf Hitler. Gran did whatever he said because it was the only way — he'd smack her, otherwise. The only say she had was what she cooked and baked, but not even that always. If he told her the pie was too spiced, she had to fix it next time. Gramp was the dictator of the house.

There was a man over in Hanover who got in the paper for saying Hitler was right about some things, like how Jews were a problem. Gramp agreed about that. He said Jews control the banks. He said Germans and Jews and all kinds got killed in the war, just because it's war.

Cam looked at a picture book in the library. They don't let people take it out but it shows the pits full of dead Jews and the bulldozers pushing the skinny bodies and the gas chambers and the ovens with burnt skeletons. Cam told Gramp about the book at supper and Gramp said the pictures were fakes.

Afterward Cam went out to the middle of the soybean field and lay down. He looked at the stars and he wondered why there were people like Hitler and Gramp. He used to talk to God in his mind, or maybe just to the universe. He still tells Dorie there's a God. That's the right way for little kids, before they can understand things. Looking at the night sky still makes him think there could be a God, until he thinks a little more. The Earth, with all its problems, is nothing. It's about as important to the whole universe as one single grain of sand out of all the sand on all the beaches in the world. Or not even.

Cam reads mostly adventure books and science books and science fiction. He's got five *Empire Annual for Boys* books his Uncle Earl gave him, plus astronomy and geology books he got from church white-elephant sales and other ones Wes got him for Christmas. He can name all the planets in order, from the sun out to Pluto, and a lot of the moons, too, but he still mixes up which moons are around which planets. He tried to teach Dorie the planet names, but she gave up after a few tries.

Dorie still hasn't been to school. Wes said Cam can home-teach her reading and writing until he figures out what to do about her education. They have to be careful about mixing with outsiders.

They're going into Wingham after lunch, him and Wes and Dorie. If he goes in with Wes, they have to take Dorie too. They have to get to the bank before three, then they'll hop over to Goderich and the new Dominion Store to stock up. Wes will park in the shade and Dorie will stay in the car with the windows cracked. If she comes with them in the supermarket, she gets really annoying and people stare. She likes the car, anyway. They let her take Cheezies and her Barbie. She knows to keep all the doors locked in case of kidnappers, like what happened to the girl in a car outside the 4-H Hall in Paisley.

On the way back they'll get some steaks and chops and sausages at Elora Road Meats and maybe a fresh chicken from Ferguson's, down the road. All the kitchen cooking is Cam's department now, but Wes cooks the steaks on a little BBQ he got at the hardware. They didn't have steak ever before because of the expense. Tonight they'll have steaks and corn and Cam will cut up Dorie's meat for her like usual. She won't even try to cut it herself. She'd just fill up on corn.

It's hard to believe this is their life. It seems almost like something bad has to happen soon. They still eat in the same kitchen at the same old table with the blue-and-yellow oilcloth and Gran's pots hanging in their exact spots like always, but now they laugh and joke. Sometimes they have spats, usually because of Dorie, but it's like nothing. No one is yelling, or hardly ever. No one gets a backhand across the face or their dinner taken away and fed to Sport, their dog who died. That was the one time they saw Gramp sad instead of angry or irritated. He looked sad after Gran died, too, but not as much. He was sad that no one cooked his dinner anymore.

Gran and Gramp used to let Dorie do what she wanted, mostly. They hardly paid her any heed except if she got really bad, Gran spanked her with the paddle. Gran called her a little gypsy. The thing was that Gran and Gramp never really wanted Cam or Dorie. Why Cam got beat so much made no sense to him, because Dorie was the wild one. But she was just a little kid and Gramp thought she was funny. The worst he gave her was a smack across the bum if she got too lippy or crazy-acting.

Cam's got a dozen ears of corn in his bucket now, enough for lunch and supper. He comes out from the row and sees Wes over by the house, talking with Doug Johnstone. Cam knows he's a Johnstone brother from the truck, and Doug from the paunch. Before he can get over to them, Doug is wheeling around and down the drive with his tires kicking up gravel. He gives Cam a wave. They don't see the Johnstones much, unless it's on a tractor in the field.

Wes looks strange, like real worried: "They want Gramp."

"Jeez, Wes."

"Yah."

"Why?"

"Want to renegotiate the lease. Doug said the yield is down."

"Doesn't look that way."

"Soybeans are down he says, two years."

"Well, you can do the lease, Wes — why not?"

"Guess I'll have to."

"What'd you tell him?"

"Told him Gramp is sick."

"Why'd you do that?" Cam hears his voice rising.

"So they'll just think the usual, that he's drunk, or sleeping it off."

"And then what? When they come back."

Wes thinks a moment. "We can say he's gone. Away. To his brother's place."

"His brother — you mean Uncle Earl?"

"That's it. No. Has to be another brother."

"But there's only Uncle Earl, Wes, that's all."

"Right. So, we can't even say where he is. Some brother we never heard of."

Cam mulls this over. "We gotta bury him. We gotta get him buried far away somewhere, or burn him or something."

"Right. That's right."

Cam stares at the house, at the cold-room window. He can see the fan spinning. "Wes?"

"Hm?"

"The truck. We gotta start up the Dodge pickup and get rid of it. Otherwise, how did Gramp go away?"

"Bus."

Cam just looks at him.

"Okay," says Wes, "the Dodge, too."

"When's Doug coming back?"

"Saturday morning."

"Two days."

"Not even." Wes stares at the ground awhile. "Burn him. That's the best way. Down by the marsh. At night. Soak that tarp with gas."

"Fire'll be too obvious at night, Wes. In the day's better. Just like someone's burning trash."

"That's exactly it. You said it. Burning trash."

"And then we have to bury the ashes. In the marsh."

They stare over the cornfield, rising in a hump then falling away to a view of the woods just past the marsh. Down there, Cam knows, is invisible, unless you're standing on the hump of the field or right down by the woods. Smoke coming up in the middle of the day would mean Gramp burning something. Like he did now and then. You never have to worry about a ground fire down by the marsh.

"Time we got rid of the bugger, anyway," says Wes. He blows out his lips. "You get lunch on. I'll run out and get a couple cans of gas from the Esso."

They barely taste their corn and sliced ham. They explain to Dorie. Dead people get burned sometimes so they don't have to get buried. Now it's time to burn Gramp.

"Where do you burn him?"

"Bottom of the north field."

"How d'ya do that?"

"We cart him out there, Dor, in Wes's car."

"Or in the truck," says Wes. "We could burn the truck, too. Like an accident. Gas cans exploded or something."

✿

It being August and mid-afternoon, the cold room is an oven under the tin roof. Cold means October to April. They store their apples and squash and potatoes until the hard freeze creeps in. Right now it feels hot enough inside to bake a pie. Gramp is no apple pie, but he must be pretty well baked by now. Wes is standing by the tarp held down with bricks. Cam still wonders why he weighed it down that way, like he thought Gramp might come to life again.

They get the bricks cleared off and they stand there. Moving the bricks seems to make a different smell come out, not the dry-rot summer smell.

"We slide the tarp off just slow and easy, then we roll him on top of it. Got that?"

"Sure, Wes."

"Take hold of the other end there."

They get the tarp off. The smell is stronger but not too bad. It's like a long-time-dead raccoon you find in the barn, fur and bones and a stink. Wes wrapped Gramp tight. He's rolled up in black plastic and tied with rope. Looks like a mummy. The cement floor around him has a stain, like maybe he leaked out of the wrapping.

"Go get some work gloves, Cam. The heavy leather ones."

With the gloves on, they roll Gramp onto the tarp. The patch of floor right underneath him is black liquid, like when potatoes go rotten. Same smell. The black stuff smears onto their gloves and the tarp when they roll him. Cam is trying hard not to breathe.

"Jesus, what a friggin' stink. Jesus H ... Push him."

"I'm pushing him, Wes."

"Push!"

They get Gramp on the tarp and roll him up in it, then they go quick out the side door to the yard. They're sweating and gulping air. Cam stares at the fields baking in the sun and the faraway woods down by the marsh where they're about to burn him.

They already got the pickup going after lunch with a boost from Wes's car. Took a while, but now it's running, parked a few feet from them, blowing black smoke out the tailpipe. Wes jammed a hunk of firewood over the gas pedal to keep it revving fast so it won't stall. The tires are half-flat but they'll do for a trip down to the marsh. Now they've got to go back inside there with the godawful smell and drag the tarp out. Dorie is on the back porch playing and pretending not to watch them. Wes told her she had to stay there.

They get Gramp out to behind the truck. He's pretty heavy, more than Cam expected. Wes stands there, thinking a moment. He pulls off a glove and shakes the other one onto the ground. He gets some more rope from the barn and ties up the tarp tight so Gramp can't spill out. Then they heave him up and into the truck bed. Cam is choking on exhaust smoke and Gramp stink. They get into the cab and Wes drives round the house and to the track running north alongside the field. Last time Cam was in the Dodge, it was Gramp driving. Looks like the same dead flies still sitting there at the corner of the dashboard. Cam opens the glovebox and there's the old Kerr's Scotch Mints tin, full of Eddy strike-anywheres.

"We're set, Wes."

"Eh?"

Cam pops the lid and shows him the matches.

They roll Gramp out the truck bed onto the spongy ground at the burning place. Wes splashes a full can of gas over the tarp. He steps back and throws a lit match at it, and then two or three more before it goes up in a whoosh of flame and gassy hot air blowing back at them. They watch the edge of the canvas start to curl up, glowing hot orange.

Then someone comes out of the woods. He's still on the other side of the swampy stretch but he's already circling round to the path that leads over the creek bed and right past them. Cam says his name before Wes.

"Jeez, it's Kyle McKieran. What's he doing in the woods?"

Cam sees he's carrying a rabbit by the ears. Blood is bright on its fur and Kyle's got a trap in the other hand. He keeps coming right at them with a stupid grin until he's not even twenty feet away.

"Whatcha burnin' today?"

"Trash. Whatcha think?"

They all stand there and watch Gramp's canvas and plastic coffin burning. The canvas disintegrates fast into glowing ash that flies up and the black plastic is melting and flaring with thick smoke curling off it, blowing over Cam and Wes. They circle round to where Kyle is staring at the fire like an idiot.

Cam says, "Nice-looking rabbit, Kyle. Where'd you get that trap?"

"Buncha them in the barn. Nearly took my hand off getting 'em set, but I got the hang of it. I'll loan you one if you want."

"Could I come get it now?"

"You can take this one. I got the rest set out in the woods."

Cam takes the trap and grins at Kyle like he's all grateful and it's a big deal.

Wes says, "You boys head up now. I'll watch this."

Kyle doesn't move. He's staring at the fire. Cam stares, too. The burning thing is human shaped now. Toe bones are sticking up and the other end is the flaming head. The top of the head flares up sudden like dry straw and they're looking at patches of white bone with the ashes of Gramp's hair floating off.

They all stare. It's like nobody can speak. The ground all around Gramp is blazing and Cam thinks, "Wreathed in fire," words from some book. Gramp's skull is wreathed with flames. The puckered skin on his face is crackling and roasting. Then there's a sound like a stick breaking. The skull splits open and rotten brain bubbles out and sizzles on the hot bone.

"Ho-ly ..." says Kyle, real quiet.

THEY'VE GOT KYLE SAT DOWN in the kitchen. Cam thinks he looks like a stunned cow with his big square head and bugging-out eyes and little wisps of red hair on his chin. Wes invited him up to the house. They had to walk back because they already shut down the Dodge they were planning to burn.

Wes says, "Will you take a glass of cold milk, Kyle? We got chocolate or regular."

Kyle asks for chocolate, but when Wes swings open the fridge door, Kyle says, "Or I'll take one of them Black Horse, if it's okay."

"Think you're legal?"

"Drank some at my friend's place anyway."

"Well, can't hurt. I see how you might want one after that campfire."

Wes says it sort of like a joke, but nobody laughs. Kyle just sits and stares with his mouth hanging open, rolling his eyes around. Then Dorie comes in and Kyle has something else to stare at.

Wes says, "Dorie, go play outside — we got business with Kyle here." Dorie just stares back at Kyle. "Out!"

Dorie wanders out like it's her own idea. They hear her singing to herself on the porch.

Wes gets two beers and pulls out a chair across from Kyle. Cam sits, too. He's trying to look relaxed. They're all sweating from the walk up but it's more than that. They've got to pretend it's all normal, like there's nothing strange about burning your Gramp. Wes is looking sad, but regular normal sad. He raises up his beer and says, "To Gramp." Kyle just watches him. "Cremation," Wes says. "Couldn't let it wait any longer."

Wes drinks and Kyle drinks and they set their bottles down.

Wes says, "Gramp always wanted his ashes here. To stay here on his land. We wanted it private. Just a shame you happened along, Kyle. Not a pretty thing to see."

From Kyle's face, you can tell he's seeing the fire again. Cam is seeing it, too. It doesn't seem real now. But he's still got the burning smell on his clothes.

"Never seen something like that. Whatcha call it again?"

"Cremation."

"My dad was buried."

They wait for Kyle to say more. He's looking like he might, but then he just takes a slug of his beer.

Cam says, "How'd your dad die, Kyle? Guess he was young, eh?"

"Highway crash. He's buried in Lucknow. That's where it happened. How'd your grandpa die?"

"You want to know how he died, Kyle?" says Wes. "You really wanna know? Too much rye whisky. So you remember that. Stick to beer."

Kyle nods and stares a long time at the floor. "He didn't burn too good, did he."

"Not the bones. Bones burn slow. When he cools down, we'll bury him in the marsh. It's what he wanted and we'll do it just like he said."

"Jeez."

"What Gramp told us to do is not the usual thing, Kyle. It's maybe not even legal. Like I said, he wanted it private. So don't go telling your mother or anyone else, got that?"

Kyle doesn't say anything.

"You got that?"

"Sure. I got it."

"It's just respect for a dying man's wishes. We don't want them coming in to dig him up with a lot of horseshit about proper burial and such."

"Okay."

"And you go ahead and keep on with your traps in our woods, just so long as you don't advertise it. Don't need half the county in here, trapping our rabbits. That a deal?"

"Yes, sir."

"Okay, then, we're settled. Drink up. Think you better get that rabbit skinned. Take a few ears of corn to go with it, if you like. We won't let on to your mother that you been drinking here."

"Thank you, sir."

Kyle finishes up his beer and they all go out to the porch, where Dorie is sitting on the step babbling something about seagulls in a funny voice and banging her heels and acting like no one else is there. They watch Kyle walk away with the dead rabbit swinging until he disappears into the corn rows.

Cam turns to Dorie. "Dorie, just button it, will you? What are you friggin' on about?"

"Red skeleton."

"What?"

Dorie shouts, "RED SKELETON."

A taste is coming up in Cam's throat. He goes back in the house and heads up the stairs to the bathroom. He has to move fast but he gets there in time and upchucks into the toilet: bile and corn and chewed-up ham.

✻

"We can't leave him, Cam. We got to go down there and get him in the marsh, at least."

"Burn the truck, too."

"Course we burn the damn truck, whatta you think?"

"Just saying, Wes. You don't need to snap."

"Who's snapping?"

"Can you get some extra gas, do you think? Maybe burn Gramp better?"

"You're a smart one today."

"You were thinking smart, too, Wes, with Kyle."

"He better not talk."

"He won't. We just got to hope not, anyway."

Wes drives out for more gas. Cam walks down past the field to the burning place. Gramp is white bones and black pieces of the rest of him stuck to the bone. If he was only ashes, they could spread him all over and then it wouldn't even matter if Kyle talked. They could make him out a liar.

Cam looks away so he won't feel sick. Way out to the east past the McKierans', he sees the giant elm tree that's been out there forever. Biggest tree for miles, all by itself in the middle of a field. Always been there, not another tree anywhere near it. Cam always thinks he'd like to go to it, be there right up close and get to know it. Looking way up the thick, tall trunk into the green leaves. The canopy. Then he remembers Gran's joke from when the Queen was on TV. She said the Queen has a canopy over her bed, but our can-o-pee is under the bed. It was like that when Gran got married to Gramp, before the indoor plumbing. She said that's what the old stain is on the sitting room ceiling. Spilled pee.

The sun is low and still hot and the air's not moving at all. There's the swampy smell mixed with the burn smell and Cam's feeling like he could puke again. He goes and sits in the dry grass far away from Gramp and stares at some black ants doing ant things, like there's no humans at all in the world. Just a busy ant world. Until a tractor runs over them.

Wes comes and he soaks the bones with gas and lights up Gramp again. Then he takes a piece of rag and rams it with a stick down the pipe to the Dodge's gas tank. He leaves it hanging out the pipe and pours some more gas over it. He soaks the cab with the rest of the gas and puts a match to it and then lights the rag hanging out the fill pipe and backs off a good distance with Cam right beside him. The back end of the truck explodes with a huge whumping bang of orange fire. A piece of red tail light lands in the grass right in front of them.

They stand there quiet for a long time, watching.

6

CAM SAYS *THE RED SKELTON COMEDY HOUR* is not funny at all, but it makes Dorie laugh. Dorie knows it's called Skelton, but she always says "Skeleton" anyway. Red Skeleton looks like a Gramp but he couldn't ever hurt anyone or yell. He's funny when he does the seagulls Gertrude and Heathcliff, flying around looking down at people.

She watches the seagulls that come from Lake Huron after a storm and land in the soybean field. Cam says they come to eat worms, but the worms are good for the crops and the birds are just pests. But Dorie likes them. They even come close to her if she goes out in the field and just sits there quiet and waits. They come and look right at her because they're curious and like to watch people, just like Gertrude and Heathcliff. They're smarter than other birds.

Dorie is out in the field now after the rain. It's wet but still warm and the sun comes out and makes steam in the air around her. The wet earth and soybean plants smell good. She has a straw hat from the pump shed and she put on a T-shirt and some shorts. The hat is too big but it's okay. She has a Tupperware full of Cheezies and she is completely happy. The seagulls are here. They are all around in the field and in the sky. If they poo, she's protected by the hat and she keeps the lid on her Cheezies when she isn't taking one out to eat it.

The field has a bump in the middle and it's the best place to sit and watch. She feels like she is the centre of the world. She has enough Cheezies to stay a long time. She makes them last. The only thing that isn't perfect is the manure spreader driving back and forth at the McKierans'. It's far away but it's throwing up cow manure behind it like a dirty brown cloud and the smell sometimes blows over her spot. It's probably Kyle driving.

She doesn't like Kyle. Not since he showed her his pee-pee and wanted to play with her in his barn. His mother came in and she screamed at Dorie and sent her home. Boys do funny things. Kyle said they had kittens in their barn, but he lied.

She turns now so she can't see the spreader but it's still stinky. Anyway, she will just ignore it.

The seagulls like Cheezies. She fed them once but they fought with each other. Now she takes out just one Cheezie at a time and pops it fast into her mouth. The birds are watching her but mostly they are eating worms or just flying around. They look really big up close and their beaks are yellow. Dorie knows they're afraid of her. If they come too close, she just stands up and scares them.

Dark clouds are coming over again and some big drops of rain fall and make plops on her hat and on the soybean leaves. She hears the thunder coming back. She doesn't mind the rain as long as she has a hat. If it gets cold, she can go back to the house, but every day is hot now. The big drops come a bit more and then they stop. The air is not moving and she can smell the plants now and not the manure smell.

They get big storms when it's hot. Sunny then stormy then sunny again. She asked Cam how so much water comes from the sky. Cam explained to her. The water from Lake Huron goes up in the clouds and they grow big with all the water and they blow over the land and dump it on the crops. That's why it's farmland. Good soil and good weather, Cam said.

The air is perfectly still. The seagulls are hardly moving now. They just turn their heads, watching. Then they all flap together and fly up and disappear into the sky. Dorie has nothing to watch, just the clouds and the manure spreader bumping along like a giant bug on its funny wheels. Then everything is bright white and a spear of lightning is stabbing into the spreader. There's a noise like her head is splitting, like the world is splitting. Then it's quiet and normal again except she's seeing things different. The lightning spear is like a blinking shadow, floating away. The spreader is still moving. It goes to the end of the field and keeps going down to the creek by the woods, bump, bump, bump, and then it stops and falls over sideways.

Dorie's ears are ringing. She stands up and she hears someone calling. Cam is in the yard, yelling at her to come in. Then the rain comes, hard and cold.

She wonders if Kyle is dead. He must be dead because he got hit by lightning and crashed right into the creek. Someone will find him there later, all rotten. She can't tell anyone. Maybe it wasn't Kyle, but if Kyle was dead, she wouldn't mind.

Cam hurt her arm dragging her into the house. He told her never, ever to go in the field when it's storming.

"I didn't!"

"You were out there, Dor. Don't lie. I saw the lightning, too."

"It was sunny!"

"You hear thunder, you get back to the house or the barn. Got it?"

"I was coming!"

"Don't backtalk me. You want the paddle?"

Cam and Wes never use the paddle on her. They just say they will. Now Cam tells her about somebody on his roof in Walkerton, he got hit by lightning and he was burned all over. He makes her promise she won't go out when it's storming.

"You shouldn't eat Cheezies all day, either. You'll turn into a Cheezie!"

"That's stupid."

"Jeez, Dorie, look at you. Go clean the mud off yourself."

✤

Wes waits for the ringing to stop. They're just finishing up supper and Cam is over at the fridge with the phone right there on the wall and he finally reaches for it.

"Leave it, Cam."

But the ringing goes on and on. Wes swears and gets out of his chair. He lifts the receiver and he can hear the voice already. He stands listening to the neighbour woman jawing away at him. He can hardly get a word in. When he hangs up, he says to Cam, "Kate McKieran. Says Kyle and Tom got hit by lightning this aft. They're in hospital."

"Holy ... Dorie was out there, too."

"Yah. Maybe they took the hit for her."

"How they doing?"

"Kyle got burnt. She said one arm, he just can't move it at all. Nerve damage."

Cam turns to Dorie, who's eating her Neapolitan ice cream and humming some tune like she's deaf to the world. "Did you hear that, Dorie? You hear what happens with lightning?"

"She said Tom saw Dorie out there. Wants to know if we saw anything. Says the boys were out in the wreck a couple hours before they found them."

Cam flares up. "What were they doing out in a friggin' storm?"

"That's it. She likely sent 'em out there herself. Dorie, you see the boys out there?"

"Nope, I never."

"Well, good, then. It's not our concern, anyway. Guess we're lucky you're not in hospital, too."

"Or dead, even," says Cam.

Dorie calmly eats the ice cream like she's really concentrating on the taste.

The phone starts up again and keeps on going and they just let it ring until it stops.

7

WHEN THE STORM CAME UP, Wes stepped out of the barn to take a look. He saw the spreader over there and he almost laughed. Storming on and off all day, and goddamn Kyle and Tom out there with the mobile lightning rod. Wes just went back into the barn kind of shaking his head. Doug Johnstone should've known better than to hire those boys.

This morning he's already come down first thing to double-check on Gramp's remains. Just in case the marsh decides to give up its dead while Doug and Roy Johnstone are out looking over their wrecked spreader. With the burnt Dodge down there, too, they're liable to hang around and gawk. Let them. He's got the story all set. He already told Doug that Gramp went away to his brother's, no idea when he'll be back. The truck? Had to be kids. Hooligans. Tools went missing from the pump shed, too. What can you do? The Dodge was ready to be junked, anyway. Don't know how they even got it started.

Doug phoned early to say they'd be coming round to winch out the spreader from the creek bed and might need his help. Wes said right away what a shame it was, the whole thing. Then he went down to make sure no bones were poking out of the marsh mud. Now he's waiting. He wants Doug and Roy to see him giving the burnt-out Dodge a going-over so they see he's got nothing to hide. When they come over the hill he'll have his head under the hood, salvaging parts.

So that's what he's doing when they come down on their new John Deere, all glossy green and yellow paint with hardly a scratch. They stop by the gap-through to the next field and they hop off the tractor like they own the whole county but know how to be nice about it. Doug is fatter than ever and Roy with the same stubble beard like a fungus got his face. Never has a real beard or a proper shave, either. Wes keeps his face clean. Cam, too.

Doug waddles over and stares at the truck's fried engine and Wes cranking a bolt off the valve cover. "Won't she start?"

Wes comes up. "Been trying all morning."

"Looks like this wire here got burnt a bit."

"You're a live one this morning."

"This thing your old Dodge?"

"That it is."

"Sam torch it before he took off?"

Wes stares at Doug's sweaty pink face. "Now why would he do that?"

"Just joking, Wes."

Doug has a milky smell. He always does. Like warm milk just starting to sour.

Wes hefts his wrench and wipes the sweat off his brow. "Gotta be kids. Found it down here day before yesterday. They got in the pump shed, too — stole some tools."

"You gonna report 'em to OPP?"

"Frig, what for, Doug?"

"You're right on that."

Roy is leaning on the idling tractor, rolling a cigarette and watching them. He's the quiet one. Says *Yep* a lot. *Yep, could be. Could be, yep.* But he's not stupid, Wes knows that.

Doug says, "A shame about those boys. Wasn't us sent them out there yesterday. We brought the spreader in a week ago."

Roy says, "They picked their time, didn't they. Field's not even half-done now."

Wes is thinking that could be the longest thing he ever heard Roy say.

"Well, let's look at the damages," says Doug, and he waddles back to the Deere and hoists himself up in the driver's seat and Roy climbs up behind. They jolt off through the windbreak and down the track to the creek.

Wes turns and stares at the truck engine. Not a single part of it anything but scorched scrap metal. He can see how he looked pretty funny struggling with the wrench.

Next morning, Doug's on the phone again.

"Wes, I can show you the figures. Soybeans was down last year near twenty-five percent and this year we got a problem with must, don't know if you noticed."

"That's about every year, Doug."

"Yah but worse, is what I'm saying, obviously."

"Uh-huh."

"Corn is looking fair but still early to get a bead on that, so what we're thinking is, don't want to be unreasonable, what say we drop the lease amount by twenty percent, renegotiate next year. Sound good?"

"I'm wondering what Sam would say, Doug."

"He'd be telling us to go elsewhere and he'd be losing. No one else around here will give you better, you know that. We been paying a generous rate to you folks three years now."

"Let me think it over."

"Sure. We'll hold the September cheque, then, till you decide."

"I'll call you before then."

Wes hangs up. He stares at the list of numbers tacked to the wall beside the phone. Been there with the same numbers on it forever. One of them is the co-op office in Walkerton. They could give him the real figures on crop yields. But he's heard that soy's been down in the whole region this year. Well, frig it. Doug wouldn't risk losing Bliss land. He's likely bluffing. Or isn't.

8

DORIE HAS A JIFFY AND grape jelly sandwich with a glass of chocolate milk. She's got her blue shorts on and a T-shirt because Cam made her. He put her sandwich on a plate and told her to sit at the kitchen table and be quiet. He's talking to Mrs. McKieran in the sitting room. Cam closed the door so Dorie can't hear anything. He forgot to cut the sandwich in triangles like he always does. Dorie drinks her milk through the bendy straw, just little sips. She's looking at the sandwich that she can't eat. She could go get a knife from the drawer.

The sitting room door bangs open. Mrs. McKieran goes straight through and out the porch way. Cam comes in the kitchen all upset. He's moving around like he can't figure where to go. He punches the fridge. He's red and breathing like Yosemite Sam mad at Bugs Bunny. He pulls out a chair and sits down. He's staring at the table and calming down. He looks at Dorie, then he looks down at her sandwich. He reaches his arm over and opens the drawer and gets a knife and he pulls Dorie's plate over and cuts up the sandwich, chop, chop, and shoves it back. The jelly and peanut butter are squeezing out the sides.

"Dorie."

"What?" Dorie dips her finger in the jelly and licks it.

"Did you go over by the McKierans' without your pants? And do dirty things?"

"I never."

"Kyle's mum says you went in their barn with Kyle."

"I never."

"Well, she's a witch. She said you did stuff. Friggin' Kyle. He's the dirty one. FRIGGIN' KYLE. FRIG HIM TO HELL."

Cam jumps up. He walks around the table and sits down again.

"Dor, I don't care what you did or what that witch lady said — just do not go there again and don't go anywhere with Kyle or Tom. Anywhere. Okay?"

"I never did nothing."

"Eat your sandwich."

"Witch lay-deeee," says Dorie with a singsong.

"God'll punish us is what she said. All of us. She's a friggin' nutcase. She says the lightning was a sign from God."

Dorie picks up a triangle of sandwich and bites into the soft bread and gooey filling. "Why will God punish us?"

"He won't, Dor — not really."

"He struck Kyle and Tom with the lightning."

"That's what their nutty mum thinks, but she's mental."

"I saw it."

"You did? Really?"

"Yip. They went and crashed down the creek and everything."

"Dorie. How come you didn't tell me?"

"Um, I was scared." Dorie bites again and her mouth fills with the goo and the peanut jelly taste.

Cam is staring at her. "When someone gets hurt, you're supposed to go tell a grown-up."

"I hate Kyle. I hate Mrs. McKieran."

"Uh-huh. Well, what did he do?"

"He showed me his pee-pee. It was big. He looked at my bum."

"Jeez, Dorie, everyone sees your bum, anyway, don't they. You went over there without your clothes?"

"I never. Kyle said to take my pants off and then the witch lady came."

"We got to change some things around here. You're not a baby. Maybe you could chew with your mouth closed, too."

"Why-yy?"

"You're gonna get it, Dor. You wait and see."

Wes comes in from shopping. He puts the grocery bags on the table and Cam starts putting the groceries away and Wes splashes his face from the tap. He gets a Black Horse from the fridge and sits down.

Dorie says, "Can you peel the label?"

Wes looks at her. "How many you got of those, Dor? You really need another one?"

Dorie likes to stick the Black Horse pictures on the closet door in the bedroom. She already has a bunch of them with the horses all going the same way. But Wes is thinking about something. The way he's looking. Looking somewhere not in the room.

He says, "That woman phone again?"

"Jeez, Wes ..."

"What, she did?"

"She phoned and she came over. Like for a chat."

"SHE LIED ABOUT ME."

"Shut it, Dorie."

Wes looks at the ceiling. He's smiling like he smiles when he's mad.

Cam says, "Dorie, go outside."

"What for?"

"Go!"

Dorie goes out to the porch. She hears Cam shutting the kitchen window so she can't listen. She sits on the porch step. She can smell the fields. A warm green smell. She takes Barbie's head out of her pocket and does the squeezing thing that makes her face so weird, like really skinny or squashed flat so her eyes and nose disappear. Then she pulls down her pants and sits down her bum right on Barbie's face. It feels funny.

She can hear Wes and Cam in the kitchen. They're talking loud but not really yelling. It's about Kyle McKieran and the barn and about Gramp, too. It's all because of the witch lady, Mrs. McKieran. It's stupid because it doesn't matter because Gramp is dead. He's not anywhere anymore. He's just a skeleton in the marsh.

Dorie comes off the porch with Barbie's head and goes and pushes it back on her neck sticking out of the ground under the maple tree. Then she hears the screen door creaking open. Cam comes out and stands on the porch.

"What you doing with that doll? You don't get a new one if you wreck it."

"She's not wrecked."

"You're a weirdo, Dor."

Cam walks up past the roses and the pumphouse and goes inside the barn. Dorie stares at the barn door, just a dark hole. People disappear. Cam was there and now he's gone. She looks at things. At the house and the grass and the roses and the corn and the sky. Just blue. No clouds. She looks at all the sky and sees some little white clouds far away. She hears banging from the barn. Cam is still inside there.

WES SCATTERS A LITTLE BLOOD meal and gives the vegetable patch a long soak, then he gets a basket from the shed and picks apples until he's got a few pounds. The sun's murder today, not a breath of wind. He's got sweat running in his eyes and feels almost dizzy when he heads back to the house. In a couple months, they'll be getting frost. He comes in and drops the basket on the kitchen floor. Cam's at the table, reading a book.

"We need some pies. Can you do that?"

"You know I never made pie."

"Just do like Gran did. I'll get what you need."

"Not that easy, Wes. Making the dough ..."

"Use a book."

"A cookbook? She never had a cookbook."

"I'll buy you one." Wes goes to the sink and soaks a towel and rubs it over his face and neck. "Thinking we might be neighbourly to those dumb-ass boys and their mommy. Pitch in, you know? In their time of need." He takes a beer out of the fridge.

"You drinking before lunchtime now?"

"Frig if I am, it's only one."

"Okay. I guess."

"You guess." Wes raises his beer like a toast to Cam. "So what you need? Flour."

"Yeah."

"Lard."

"That's it. Maybe you can bake the pies, Wes."

"Do enough around here. What else?"

Wes watches Cam staring into space, thinking about how to make a pie. The beer is cold and yeasty. Nothing beats those first sips. Cam puts a bookmark in his book and closes it. They sit there looking at each other.

Wes says, "So? What else?"

"That's all. Flour and lard and apples and … sugar."

"Spice."

"Right, sugar and spice. We got them."

Wes is looking at Cam's face. How above his eyebrows, it kind of juts out. A ridge. Cam's got blond eyebrows, even though his hair is dark brown. Thick hair, a real mop of it. Wes is already losing his.

Cam opens his book again. Wes sees his eyes moving in little jerks across the words. He takes a slug of beer and sets the bottle down, quiet. He can smell Cam, his sweat, just regular hot-day sweat. The sweat smell is different when Cam gets fired up. Like slicing a fresh onion.

Cam looks up at him. "What you staring at?"

"You."

Cam shakes his head and goes back to reading. With his eyes on the book, he says, "There's a couple chicken legs in the fridge. I ate already."

❖

Wes gets the pie things in Walkerton, where he never goes usually. Who does he run into at the IGA but Ron and Beth Harmer,

exactly the kind of folks he's been avoiding since Gramp died. Wes
hasn't seen them for a year or two, maybe not since Gran's funeral.
Of course they ask how's things and they've been wondering where
the Bliss folks have got to and how's the old man doing these days.
Ron has that look in his eye like he's really asking, *Is he dead from
the boozing yet?* Wes says they're doing okay, just Sam is slowing
down and doesn't get out much since Alice died.

"Still in the dumps, is he?" says Beth. She has a gushy smile.
"And how are the children these days?"

"Good, thanks."

"The little one, she'd be in school soon."

"Dorie? Yah. Over in Kincardine."

"Well. That's a trek."

Ron and Beth stare at him like everyone does. Like they don't
believe a thing he says and they're sad for the kids who aren't really
proper kids and they don't approve of anything about the Bliss
family, anyway. Nothing new.

"I see you're doing some baking."

They all look down at the flour and lard in Wes's cart.

"Cam does that. Makes a real decent pie."

They just stare at him some more.

When Wes gets outside, he remembers he has to get a cookbook. Where the hell …? He waits till the Harmers come out and
get in their car and drive away, then he goes back inside the IGA.

The cashier just looks at him. "We don't carry cooking books,
sir."

"I need a baking book."

"There's Stedmans, just next door here. Or Knights of
Columbus, maybe. The thrift shop, on Colborne, two blocks over."

Wes should've thought of Stedmans. He goes in, but they don't
have it. He finds the thrift shop. They've got used books and after
a while the woman locates one called *McCurdy's Scottish Kitchen*.

"Does it have pies?"

"Well, let's look. Yes. Whole chapter on them."

Walking back, he runs into Al Shields, a fellow from back in school days, before his father moved them to Hamilton. Al was one of his best pals till he was maybe fourteen or fifteen. He's another one Wes hasn't seen for years. Christ. He knew he should've shopped in Goderich.

"Wes, you beggar. What's it been?"

"A while."

"Couple years, anyway. What're you up to?"

"Oh, this and that. Just doing a little shopping."

"You been away?"

"Nope."

"I was talking to Doug Johnstone last week. Shame what happened with the neighbour boys."

"Sure was."

"Can't say I blame Doug at all."

"He's the one hired them."

"Sam's truck got burnt too, they said."

"Yah, some crazy kids …"

"How you folks doing?"

"Okay. You?"

"I guess you didn't hear. My mother passed on."

"Jeez, I'm sorry, Al — when was that?"

"End of May. Just dropped dead making dinner."

"Jeez, that's rough."

"Got a good turnout for her anyhow. Church and school and so on. She taught your cousin Cam a few years. I guess you know."

"I didn't know that."

Al is nodding at him.

"I been out of commission, Al. Just don't get out much, hardly even look at a newspaper anymore."

"Old Sam's a handful, is he?"

"Nah, he's gone, to his brother. Gone a couple weeks now."

"That the Toronto fella?"

"Nope, not Earl. The other brother. Down Windsor way."

Al's looking at him just like the Harmers did.

❋

Cam does the pies in the Moffat. He fits in four on the two shelves and the top ones come out pretty brown looking but not really burnt. The bottom ones look better, sort of like Gran's. The pastry fell apart when he was putting it in the pans and over the apples, but he can't see how that'll change the taste. The smell in the house is just like when Gran was there, maybe even spicier. So they've got two pies for the McKierans and two for home. He knows they have to cool an hour or two, so he tells Wes to stop hanging around sniffing and staring at them.

"They're looking good, Cam. I think you got talent."

"Smell better than they look."

"It's the eating that counts."

"No pie-eating till supper. I told you they have to cool down."

"Yessir, Gran."

They look at each other a moment.

Cam says, "She did things different from the recipe book. I was remembering. So I tried to do like she did."

"Good thinking. Okay, then, I'll take two over next door. Which ones?"

"They gotta cool down, I told you."

Wes is laughing. "You're just like the old lady."

"You shouldn't call her that."

Cam's on the porch reading a Ray Bradbury story, but he can't concentrate too well because he's thinking about apple pie. It was pretty good, but next time he might put more sugar in and maybe less spice. He'll get the crust better next time, too.

Wes just went over next door with two pies for the McKierans. Cam's glad it's Wes and not him talking to Kyle's crazy mum. He sets the book aside. Right now the sun is doing a thing it does when it's close to setting. It comes in the west-facing window and shines right through the house and out the porch window. A patch of the rose bush is lit up like the sun is inside the house, shining a spotlight. The roses are glowing orange-peachy coloured. Cam sees this happen every year and only in August.

What if Kyle tells his mum about burning Gramp? She'll have a complete fit is what. She'll maybe phone the police, and the po-lice will come and ask them questions, and then what do they say?

He hears Dorie talking to herself in the kitchen. She didn't even finish her pie. Cam thinks about it. He must've doubled the sugar when he really needed to times-four it. And he put extra cinnamon and cloves because he couldn't taste it, but after it was cooked, it was too much spice taste. But with the extra sugar next time, it might be just fine.

Wes comes back from delivering the pies. He sits on the porch step and just stares and shakes his head. "That woman," he says. "And those boys." He says Kyle's left arm is completely dead. Not actual dead, just not functioning. And his face and neck all red with burns. Wes says it's good, though, since Kyle is so sick he probably forgot all about Gramp. Tom's burnt too but his arms and everything work fine.

"She takes me in where they're watching television. I swear, Cam, they looked like two imbeciles with their mouths open, star-ing at the TV. I guess they're in pain. Looks just like a real bad sunburn. I said, 'Just stopping in, see how you're doing, I brought some pies.' And Kate says, 'They won't be having pie. Spoil their dinner.'"

"She doesn't sound very thankful for fresh-baked pies."

"She hardly looked at them. Like she couldn't even see them, right there on her kitchen table."

"What's the matter with her?"

"She gave me this." Wes pulls something out of his pocket. "A track."

Cam takes the pamphlet. It's got a picture of people at a picnic with a lion and a tiger beside them on the grass. A little girl is petting the lion. There's sheep and a giraffe and monkeys in a tree and birds and flowers everywhere.

"It's a tract, Wes."

"Yah. That's Heaven, I guess."

They stare at the picture.

"Would you like another slice of pie?"

"Sure. Sure I would, Cam."

"I'll bring it out."

"What about some ice cream on it?"

"All we got's chocolate."

"That'll do fine."

Cam goes in and cuts two slices and puts ice cream on and brings them out. They sit on the wicker sofa that Gran always called the loveseat, with the plates on their knees. Cam thinks the chocolate is not the best idea, but Wes eats his all down and keeps saying how good it is. They finish up and they sit there and watch the swifts dart around in the fading light.

Wes says, "Kyle won't say a damn thing about Gramp. First, he knows his ma would have a fit. Second, it's just a crazy thing. She'd say he was making up stories."

"You're right, Wes. I mean I hope so, anyway."

"Yah."

Cam takes the plates in. Dorie is asleep on the daybed in the old kitchen. She's flat on her tummy with one arm hanging off the edge and her Barbie dropped there on the lino. Dorie is completely still, like a picture. He can't even hear her breathing. He thinks of putting the quilt over, but it might wake her up. It's too hot, anyway.

He puts his head out the porch door. "You want a Black Horse, Wes?" Wes says no thanks.

Cam washes up and when he comes out Wes has his shirt off and he's leaning against the porch post. There's a breeze coming with the field scent and the roses. Cam moves closer to Wes. He can smell his sweat. He touches his back. Wes hardly moves. Cam moves his fingers down the groove of Wes's back. His spine. Wes tilts his head back. He makes a hmm sound. Cam just keeps moving his hand slow, up to Wes's shoulders and down his spine again, down and up again, and Wes goes hmmmm some more, and while Cam's doing this he's looking at the big old elm tree way off by itself in the field. It's still got a little patch of sun on it, glowing, at the very top.

the
hell pit

10

THE CHURCH LADIES ARE SMILING at Cam through the screen door. There's a perfumey smell drifting in and they've got flowers on their dresses. Dorie is out there behind them in the yard, babbling away to herself, but it's like the church ladies are pretending she's not there. She's got a dirty face and there's SpaghettiOs on her shirt from lunch and she's playing with the pickup truck, scooping dirt into it. At least she's got pants on.

The one woman is saying all friendly, "Just a quick chat? We won't overstay our welcome."

"Okay," says Cam. "Don't think we can donate, though."

"Oh, that's not why we're here."

He leads them in through the old kitchen and into the sitting room. They look around and then sit together on the sofa at one end. They both have brown plastic folders with a gold cross on them. The brown is a fresh-cow-shit colour.

Cam sits in the chair by the TV, far away from them. They're looking around the room at everything, smiling with their lips closed tight.

The tubby one looks at Cam and says, "Would Mr. Bliss be at home?"

"You mean Gramp?"

"Yes. Your grandfather."

"He's gone."

"He's still away, then."

"Yup. Yes. He's visiting."

"Would he be close by?"

"No. It's far. Down Windsor way."

"Well, Windsor's not Timbuktu, is it. Is Wesley Cody here?"

"Gone out."

They sit staring at him.

"Cameron …"

"I'm just Cam. Everyone says Cam."

"Cam, we are volunteers with the Bruce County Children's Aid Society. I'm afraid someone has been in touch with us, a neighbour, about your situation here."

"What neighbour?"

"We can't say."

"We only got one neighbour."

"We just can't say."

"She's crazy."

"I don't think that's quite the case."

"She said God struck her sons with lightning as a warning and now Kyle can't even use his arm. That's mental if you ask me."

"They're Pentecostal. Regardless, she spoke with our branch director by phone, at quite a length. Her concern is a valid one. She in fact suggested that we inform the police. We disagreed with that, of course."

Now Cam's stomach is flipping.

The thinner woman speaks. "It's about the attire of the child."

"Dorie? You mean her clothes?"

"Her clothes. That is what 'attire' means."

The tubby woman says, "The child should be dressed. The other question is your guardianship and the child's, and her education. The society upholds basic standards —"

"We don't need Children's Aid."

"The girl does not have a mother," says the thin one, "nor do you."

"I'm seventeen, I don't need a mother. We got Wes."

"We will need to talk to Wes. And to your grandfather. Do you know how to reach your grandfather?"

"No. We don't care where he is. He can stay there."

They stare at Cam, like trying to read his mind.

Tubby says, "Why should he stay where he is, Cam?"

"I don't have to talk to you."

"There's no need to use that tone of voice."

"We don't need your Jesus stuff and we don't need a mother. If you're Children's Aid, why're you pretending to be a church?"

"Heavens, we're not pretending, we're with Bethel Baptist."

"We go to St. John's."

"Do you. Every Sunday, I suppose." The thin one snorts.

"Where is Wes now?" says Tubby.

"He won't talk to you, either."

"Did he go to Windsor, too?"

"No. It's none of your business."

The thin one says, "Young man. The welfare of children is our business. It is the Lord's business. This family, so-called, is outside the law. That means God's law and the laws of Ontario. It is just a fact. And that girl, well …"

"What'd that witch say about her? Is it about her and Kyle?"

"What about Kyle?" says Tubby.

"He took Dorie in his barn. And did stuff."

"Stuff?"

"He showed her his … his boy thing. His wiener."

Thin's mouth puckers up.

"He wanted to look at her. He's a frigging pervert."

They all sit quiet for a bit. The tubby lady gives a big sigh.

"Well, then. As Miss Gurney said, your household is not in order. The girl needs to be covered up. At all times. Kyle is a growing boy, after all, and boys are boys. Fortunately he's out of commission now. We do need to speak with an adult, either Wes or your grandpa. I'm going to give you my telephone number and you can tell Wes to call me."

Tubby writes down her number and hands it to Cam.

"It says 'Miss Gurney.'"

"Yes."

"You said she was Miss Gurney."

"She is Miss Audrey Gurney. I am Miss Beulah Gurney. Will you show us out, please?"

Dorie is on the porch. Her face looks even dirtier to Cam. The ladies walk out to their car. Cam takes a good look at it now. A two-tone Mercury, coral and blue, probably 1959, real clean and the chrome all shiny. Where'd those old bags get a car like that? Jeez, if there's a hell they can go there anytime.

Wes comes in a bit later. He gets a beer and plunks himself down at the table. Cam's right across from him, peeling potatoes, but it's like Wes's eyes go straight through him.

"I been to see Doug Johnstone."

"So?"

"So they're asking if I want work." He takes a slug from the bottle.

"What kind?"

"Whatta you think? They got an idea they pay me some crap amount to bring the corn in for them, instead of giving us proper market rate for the land it's on."

"That's crap, Wes."

"He can stick his offer up his friggin' wazoo."

"Wes, I gotta tell you something. The churchies were here. Baptist ladies."

"Uh-huh?"

"They gave me this, said you gotta phone them." Cam slides across the paper with the number.

Wes hardly looks at it. He takes a long drink of beer and asks Cam what's for supper.

"Wes. Listen. They're Children's Aid. Mrs. McKieran called them about Dorie, like she's to blame for what Kyle did."

Wes stares at him, then he closes his eyes. He starts shaking his head.

"What a load of ... And they come to us? They can go tell Kyle he's a sex pervert that diddles little girls."

"That's what I told them but they want Gramp. I said he's gone. They said Dorie has to go to school and we need a mother."

"They can go to goddamn Baptist hell. Jesus H ..." Wes gets up. He stands there staring a long time. Then he goes out.

Cam sees him from the window, walking fast down the drive.

Coming up to the McKierans' house, Wes sees their old jalopy isn't there. Just as well because if that woman was home he might get himself in too deep, he's so steamed. He goes up the steps and bangs on the sagging screen door. He's looking right into the kitchen through the screen but no one's there that he can see. A rank smell drifts out.

"Hello there! Hey!"

There's flies swarming the screen and buzzing around his head. He can see through to the hall and the stairs going up.

"Anyone home? Hey!"

"Who's there?"

The voice sounds like Kyle. Wes sees someone moving up the top of the stairs.

"It's Wes, from next door. We need to talk."

"What for?"

"I'm coming in, Kyle."

"Whatcha want, anyway?"

Wes steps in. The kitchen stinks of garbage. There's dirty plates on the table. Kyle is coming down the stairs and Wes sees his burnt arm hanging, bumping against his side. He comes along into the kitchen and stands there staring at Wes with his jaw hanging open, stains on his T-shirt.

"You alone here? Where's your mother?"

"They got a church thing in Guelph. Picnic and whatnot."

"How long's she gone?"

"Couple days. With my gramma. Tom, too."

"What're you doing here?"

"Didn't wanna go."

"Mind if I sit down?"

Wes sits. Kyle stands there watching him and says, "I didn't tell no one about the traps."

"The traps? It's not about the traps. Sit down, Kyle."

Kyle sits and they look at each other across the dirty plates, flies crawling around on the chicken bones.

"How's that arm?"

"Can't hardly move it."

"Don't think your mom should've left you here like this. Just an opinion."

"Told ya, I didn't wanna go."

Wes looks at Kyle with his hair all mussed like he just fell out of bed and his face and neck all red and scaly on one side, and the red, scaly arm hanging.

"It's a shame, Kyle, what happened to you boys."

"Guess we shoulda stayed in, storming like it was."

"I'd say so."

Kyle reaches across with his good arm and pulls the limp one up and lays it on the table. The hand is like a claw. A couple flies land on it and Kyle just looks at them.

"Kyle, your mother thinks we don't know how to run our own house or take proper care of Dorie. She got on the blower to Children's Aid and now we got Bible-thumpers coming round, nosing into our business. But you know what they said? They said we oughta keep Dorie far away from you. It was like a warning, to protect her."

"I never touched Dorie."

"What happened in the barn?"

"Nothin'. My mom didn't send no Children's Aid."

"Well, she did. But it backfired, okay. The blame is on you. And you can tell your mother that. Tell her she can't go around blabbing about our business and how we raise Dorie. That is goddamn friggin' horseshit. You are the pervert, Kyle. It's you. You can't go taking little girls in your barn just so you can get some kind of kicks."

"I didn't."

"Dorie told us what you did."

"She's a liar."

"Honestly, Kyle, you know, I can't say it. I honestly can't say the thing. But it's a sick thing, what you did to her. Disgusting is what it is."

"That's a buncha crap."

Wes stands up. "So you tell your mother I came by, and you tell her to lay off us. You got that?"

Kyle just stares with his mouth gaping.

"I said, Kyle, 'You got that?'"

"Buncha crap."

Wes goes out the screen door. He's not even down the steps and he hears Kyle shout at him.

"I know what you did! You and Cam!"

Wes keeps on walking.

• • •

Cam hears Wes come in. He finds him in the kitchen.

"It's just Kyle over there. Told him his ma's got to lay off us."

"Think you're gonna call Gurney?"

"Why should I? They can't tell us our business."

"But Children's Aid'll just come round otherwise. Official like."

"Doesn't say Children's Aid here with the number. They give you anything else?"

"Nope."

"Not so official, then." Wes looks at the ceiling, like the answer's up there. "We need to feed them a line."

Wes is thinking. He rolls his head around the way he does, making the neck bones pop.

"Here's the thing," says Wes. "You know what I told Kyle over there? I told him we know exactly what he did to Dorie. Okay, maybe it was basically peekaboo, but he doesn't know what Dorie could've said, right? I told him we know more than his mum or anyone. I said it's enough to make anyone friggin' sick, what he did."

"Like what?"

"Well, see, he's trying to figure that out. He just knows it's bad."

"Not if he didn't do it."

"Doesn't matter. It's his word against Dorie, an innocent little girl."

"But Mrs. McKieran saw them."

"When'd she come in? They coulda been at it an hour already."

"Aw, jeez."

"Kyle needs to know we got something on him. If he blabs about Gramp, police come and start nosing around ..."

"Aw, jeez, no."

"So we keep Kyle scared. The damn churchies need to know we are not the problem. Not for those nosy parkers and not for Children's Aid either, or anyone else aiming to poke around our life here. It's the damn McKierans that need Children's Aid."

"But they wanna find Gramp."

"No one's gonna find Gramp. They got me here. I'm managing the place. I'm negotiating the land, the money, the whole kit 'n' caboodle. I'm in charge now. I can show them the bank papers, too — show them Gran put me in charge."

"So you gonna call Gurney?"

"Frig Gurney. Let her come back here, we'll tell her what's what."

11

IT'S SUNDAY AND CAM'S ON the porch reading. Dorie's inside watching TV. They just finished supper and *Walt Disney's Wonderful World of Color* is on. It's still light enough to read even on the shady porch. Wes hopped over to Ferguson's to get some eggs. Cam's reading a Ray Bradbury story about a boy named Raimundo and the Day of Death in Mexico. They make skulls out of sugar and kids eat them. They're eating death. But death tastes sweet. Cam's mind is filled with pictures from the story like he's right there in Mexico with Raimundo. He can feel the sugar crunching in his mouth.

Then he hears the TV music that means Walt Disney is over. Maybe he can finish the story before Dorie comes out and bothers him. But nope, here she comes, out the door. Cam just keeps his nose in the book, but she sits on the step and bangs her heels.

"I saw horses on Walt Disney."

Cam ignores her.

"They were flying."

"It's just a cartoon."

"I know that."

"Okay, you know that."

"Horseeee …"

"Shut it, Dorie, I'm reading."

Dorie makes a big sighing noise like she's real put upon.

"Stop banging, will you? Just stop. I'm reading, okay?"

"Smell my bum."

"What?"

"SMELL MY SMELLY BUM."

"I oughta paddle you. What kinda talk is that?"

Dorie bangs her heels and keeps on talking. "God'll get Kyle McKieran. He was bad, that's why the lightning hit him. I hope he dies. Bad bad bad bad bad bad bad bad bad Kyle McKieran."

Cam looks at Dorie and says real serious, "Stop banging. Stop it. Right now." Dorie stops. "You should never say that, you hope someone dies. Even if it's bad Kyle McKieran."

Dorie tilts her head like she's thinking about it, or she's just being stubborn. She steps off the porch. She goes running in circles around the maple trees, singing Dorie nonsense. Cam watches her and he's thinking about Kyle and the barn. Dorie drops down on the grass on her back. She just lies there completely still with her eyes staring and blinking. The only thing moving is her eyelids blinking, like she's testing them or something. Cam watches and thinks how weird she is. She's always been weird.

"Tell me what Kyle did. In the barn."

The blinking stops. Dorie is quiet for a while. "He said there was kittens."

"He lied, to make you come there."

"He took his pants down. He said to show me something. He said to get bare naked. His pee-pee was big."

"Big?"

"It was sticking up."

"Sticking up? Like a pole?"

"He played with it. He said show my bum. He said to pee for him, but I didn't."

"Okay, Dorie, that's enough."

Dorie lays there quiet a moment. "He peed white stuff."

"Jeez, just shut it, okay?"

"Mrs. McKieran came and she was yelling. She hit Kyle."

"Jeez, Dorie. You're not telling tales, right? He did that."

"Yip."

"That's why his mother yelled and hit him."

"Yip. She tried to hit me but I ran away."

"Dorie, listen. You can't ever go with anyone. Not anyone. Only me or Wes. People lie. Boys do bad stuff."

"Like you and Wes."

Cam stares at her. "We don't do bad stuff. That's not true."

"Upstairs."

"We're just messing around, Dor. You're a little girl. Kyle should never've done that and he's gonna be punished."

"He can get the paddle."

"Worse, Dor. Way worse."

12

THE GURNEY SISTERS LOOK EXACTLY the same. Maybe their flowery dresses are different, but Cam can't tell. They sit the same on the sofa with Beulah at one end and Audrey right there beside her so they're almost touching. Cam thinks about Gran and how she said Nellie and Nan Ferguson were practically joined at the hip. Now there's only Nellie Ferguson, but anyhow they were never like these two.

Cam was out on the porch, catching the morning sun, and he saw a glint up by the hydro depot and there was the big church-lady Merc turning down from the Elora Road. He told Dorie right away to run to the barn, but then he changed his mind and said go down to the burning place by the marsh. They'd for sure never look there.

Wes went out early to talk with Doug Johnstone about the crops. He's not back yet and Cam hopes he comes back soon so he can show the Gurneys the bank papers that put Wes in charge. The ladies don't have their cow-shit-brown Jesus folders this time — not that it'll make a difference.

"Cameron —"

"Told you I'm Cam, just Cam, okay? And Gramp's still away."

"Wesley, then? Is he here?" says Beulah.

"Went out with Dorie."

"Course he did," says Audrey. She flicks her bony hand.

Beulah clears her throat. "Well, then. We will speak to you."

"That's real nice of you."

"Don't start your smart-talk."

"Smart? I'm just a dumb kid."

Beulah pulls a folded piece of paper out of her purse. She gives it to Audrey and Audrey gets up and holds it right in Cam's face. Cam catches an old-lady smell.

"Take it."

Cam grabs the paper.

"Can you —"

"Yes, I can friggin' read. I go the Walkerton Library. I bet I read more than you."

Audrey goes back to the sofa to join her hip to Beulah. Cam looks at the pamphlet. It says *Bruce County Children's Aid Society* across the top and underneath, *Foster Care*, but then Beulah is talking again.

"The society looked at the family history for the girl. It seems there was never an adoption, not at any time. She was born to a Mr. and Mrs. Luke Price, of Hamilton."

"You don't know anything. The Price folks were no good. Her mum was a drug addict."

Skinny Audrey says, "Well, thank goodness she's in better circumstances. No mother, an elderly man with alcoholism, and the only adult still present is without means of support. How do you expect to provide for the girl?" Her face has a twitch, like she's winking at Cam.

"We got the farm. We got support. You ask Wes. You can ask the Johnstones, too, and the Dominion Bank in Wingham."

Beulah says, "Who are the Johnstones?"

"See? You don't know much."

Audrey stands up. "Where is this Wes? In the barn? With the girl? Is he the one keeps that child out in the public eye in a state of nakedness?"

Beulah reaches out and touches Audrey's arm. Audrey sits down and starts praying. She's got her blue skeleton hands clutched together. Cam's heard of people wringing their hands but this is really it, like she might pop her bulging veins. She's mumbling Jesus stuff: *Goodness* and *Mercy* and *Dear Lord wash these sinners clean*, rocking back and forth with her eyes squeezed shut. She just keeps on going and meantime Beulah's got a weird smile stuck on her face.

"Audrey. Audrey dear. Go to the car now. Go and sit in the car. I'll come out."

Audrey gets up. She goes out the sitting room door with her hand over her mouth. Beulah waits until they hear the car door clunk shut.

"Holy ... What's wrong with her?"

Beulah looks at her hands for a long time. She's holding them in her lap and kind of wringing them, but nothing like her loony sister.

"She has been tested."

"Tested?"

"As a child. Tested."

"Like for rabies?"

"It's to do with sin. What sin of the flesh leads to, if left to run its course."

Beulah looks at Cam like she wants to go right inside his head.

"I will ask you a question, Cam. Have you ever in your life, even once, had carnal relations?"

"Dunno what you mean."

"Well, then, did you ever show Doric your boy thing?"

"Why would I do that?"

"Why would Kyle McKieran do it? Why was that girl abducted from the 4-H Hall in Paisley? Why would men in Toronto pick up teenage boys in the bus station and molest them in a hotel across the street, a place known to be a flophouse for deviants?"

"That happened in Toronto?"

"People have lost the fear of damnation. But it's real. Hell is a real place."

There's a sound outside, the car door again. Beulah gets off the sofa and goes out. Cam starts reading the pamphlet they gave him. What it says is they can put kids in foster care if they have "just cause in the interest of the child." They can take Dorie away.

❖

Everything in the truck is burnt. The seat is just springs. The glass is all broken and scattered in little pieces. Dorie stares all around but there's no bones. Wes and Cam said bones don't burn but she can't see Gramp. She wanted to see his skeleton like he was sitting in the truck.

She sits in the tall grass by the windbreak and thinks about the burning. Gramp couldn't sit in the truck because he was dead and he was all wrapped up in the tarp. But seeing his bones sitting up in the seat, that would be funny.

How long does she have to stay here? She gets up and wanders down to the marsh and walks around to where the long plank goes across the creek. It's just one skinny plank and it bends in the middle but she doesn't have to use it anyway, the creek is almost dry. She steps across on the flat stones and along the path into the woods where she didn't go for a long time because she's not allowed unless Cam is with her. But now she's older, she's nearly six, and nobody's watching, anyway.

The path goes in through the trees like she remembers. There's the same big rock with the sparkle bits and then it gets shady and sometimes there's poison ivy off the path, so she won't go there. She got it once. Cam put pink calamine on.

She walks to where the path goes two ways and she can't decide.

Dorie hears a noise, like an animal maybe. She looks along the two paths. On one she can see something moving. It's big and blue. It's someone in a blue shirt. The person is bent over beside a tree. She walks along watching until she's a bit closer.

"Whatcha doing?"

The person jumps up. It's Kyle McKieran! He's jumping all over and yelling. He's yelling so loud. He's got a thing hanging on his hand. Dorie knows what it is but she can't remember the word. They were in the McKierans' barn. They're for catching ... rabbits. Rabbit traps.

Kyle stops jumping around. He's breathing funny. "Crikey, help me. Get it off me."

Kyle's other arm is hanging down. He swings it but it only falls back and hangs there. It's really strange. The arm with the trap is bleeding. The blood is running down Kyle's hand.

"HELP ME."

Dorie can't help. It's too scary and she'll get Kyle's blood on her and Kyle should just die anyway. Why didn't God kill him with the lightning? She goes back out of the woods and across the creek and up along the windbreak, singing about Kyle dying until she can see the church ladies' car. Then a lady comes out of the house. Dorie goes right away behind the woodpile and when she can't see the lady, she goes in the barn — but the other lady is inside! The skinny one. She points at Dorie.

"You. You."

Dorie runs out. She runs straight into the cornfield and keeps going along the row until she's far in the middle and can't hear the lady yelling.

❋

Cam stares at the pamphlet. It would be the worst if they took Dorie. Would they give her to the Gurney sisters for foster parents? He's thinking that's exactly what the sisters want. They want to make her wear stupid girly dresses and go to Baptist Sunday school.

She'll tell them all about Gramp, and what Cam and Wes do upstairs. Cam feels sick in his stomach thinking about it.

He goes outside and sees the ladies over by the barn. Why can't they just leave? Audrey the loony is waving her arms around.

Now there's someone coming out around the east side of the field. It's Kyle. He's got a rabbit trap and blood all over him. The trap is — holy — the trap is on him; it's clamped on his arm.

Kyle keeps coming, right up to Cam. Sweat is running down his face. "Get it off me."

Cam stares at the blood, so much blood, all over Kyle's pants and dripping off the trap.

"GET IT OFF ME, THE RELEASE, PUSH THE RELEASE."

Cam sees a lever thing. He takes hold and wiggles it until the trap springs open and clangs to the gravel. Kyle holds up his hand and they're staring at the blood still coming out of his wrist, then his eyes go white and he drops flat out on the ground.

Cam hears Beulah beside him.

"Your shirt, tie it on his arm. Quickly!"

Cam tugs off his T-shirt. He knots it tight as he can above Kyle's elbow. Beulah brings her car over and they drag and lift him into the back seat. He starts to wake up. His blood is all over the seat cushions and Beulah's dress, all over Cam. Beulah gets back in the driver's seat.

"Audrey, for the love of God, get in the car. Get in the car!"

Audrey shuffles over and gets in.

Beulah looks straight at Cam. "You pray for us and for this wounded boy. And you pray for Dorie, too, and for yourself and your redemption." The way she says it is like it's actually Cam's fault that dumb Kyle is gonna get himself killed someday.

She turns the big car around and heads down the drive. Cam's thinking she could maybe go a little faster since it's an emergency.

"Is Kyle gonna die?"

Dorie's standing there on the edge of the field.

"I told you to stay down by the marsh, you little ..."

"You got blood all over."

"It's Kyle's blood. And no, he's not gonna die."

"He scared me in the woods."

"Why were you in the woods? There's traps all over down there. You could ..."

Cam is suddenly furious. He goes to Dorie and grabs her and drags her toward the house and she starts screaming, piercing his eardrums. She breaks away from him and runs to the house. She runs inside and keeps screaming like she's completely crazy. She yells through the screen door.

"KYLE McKIERAN CAN DIE GOD WILL KILL HIM FRIG HIM ANYWAYS FRIG HIS MUM AND THE CHURCH LADIES THEY CAN ALL DIE."

Dorie starts tearing around inside the house. Cam hears her knocking stuff over. He doesn't go in. It's like he's frozen. In his mind he's seeing the blood coming out of Kyle's wrist. He looks at his hands and they're sticky red with Kyle's blood.

He goes up the porch steps and inside. Dorie is on the daybed now, scrunched up quiet in the corner, watching him. Her arm has his bloody handprint on it. The tall lamp beside the sofa is knocked over and the light bulb is smashed. The table at the other end is over, too, and Cam's library books are scattered across the floor.

He goes to the kitchen sink to wash and the water runs red down the drain. He opens the broom closet and takes the paddle off the hook behind the ironing board. Dorie watches him coming. When he's right beside her, she jumps off the daybed and runs out through the cold room.

"Come back here, Dor! You little —"

But he doesn't chase her. He sits down. He sits quiet for a while. His mind is filling up with all the bad things that happen, that might happen to them. He still has the paddle in his hand. He sees some gobs of blood on his arm where he didn't wash. He stares at the blood, Kyle's blood clotted there in the blond hairs on his arm. He knows why blood clots. It's so people don't die from losing too much.

Kyle won't die, probably. Cam thinks of the rusty rabbit trap and how Kyle's wrist looked chewed, like raw meat and white gristle. The white is tendons, the strings that pull the muscles. And his other arm hanging there, stiff and red with skin flaking off. What if it was actually true? That God is punishing Kyle? First one arm from the lightning and then the other one, so he can't use his hands anymore. Can't even hold his own wiener to pee. Or eat by himself. His mum will have to feed him like a baby. But Cam doesn't believe in God. Because stuff that happens is too awful. Like what happened to the Jews.

Cam goes and washes again. He uses a scrub brush for under his nails. He puts on a fresh T-shirt and jeans. He tidies up the mess Dorie made and cleans up the broken light bulb. The lampshade is all bent now. Every time he looks at it, he'll remember this day. He's thinking, should he phone Kyle's mother and tell her? But he doesn't know what hospital they're at. And for sure he doesn't want to talk to her.

He looks up and Dorie is on the porch behind the screen, watching him. "Come in and get that blood off you, Dor."

"Why does Kyle trap rabbits?"

"For eating. What were you doing in the woods with him? Did he take you in there?"

Dorie doesn't say anything.

"Tell me, Dor. Just tell me. Don't lie."

"I saw the trap get him."

"Why'd you go in there?"
"Ummm …"
"Did he touch you?"
"I ran away."
"Get in here. I'm not gonna paddle you."

13

WES STARES ACROSS THE DESK in Doug's tin-can Quonset hut office. Doug is smirking like something's funny and he's about to start braying at Wes the way he does, like having a friggin' asthma attack. He's got a pair of needle-nose pliers he's been playing with and tapping on the metal Mack Truck ashtray that's always got a year's worth of butts in it. The desk is heavy wood like you'd see in a bank or someplace but scarred up like a workbench and covered in junk.

Wes can't see there's anything funny. "Christ, Doug. You think I want to be one of your field hands?"

Doug kind of huffs, half a laugh and half a sneer. He puts the pliers down and spins them and they rotate a few turns and point right back at him. He shoves them aside. "You're idle, Wes. Don't tell me you're not idle. Gentleman farmer, that's you."

"You saying I'm lazy?"

"I-dle. What's doing? You come into some money?"

"Matter of fact, I'm running the place. Money and everything else."

"How's that?"

"Just is. The old lady put me in charge before she passed on."

Doug stares at him. "Sam's out of the picture?"

"I'll tell you the picture, Doug. Sam is gone. He was gone before he was gone. I'm saying he did nothing twenty-four hours a day but drink and sleep it off, and then he vamoosed. He said to see his brother down in Windsor."

"Which brother is that?"

"Haven't a clue, Doug. News to me. Anyhow, I'm it now. We got the bank papers changed when he was too far gone to care. Hasn't been a picnic, I'll tell you."

Doug starts shaking his head like he's actually sad for Wes and the whole Bliss clan, which Wes knows is pure bull.

"Took you this long. All the years the old man was knocking it back and you folks thought you was covering for him. You could smell it on him, everyone could. Sitting right there where you are. Smelled like driving past Hiram Walker's." Doug chews on his lip. "You taking good care of those kids?"

"Who else? Course I take care of them."

"How's Cam doing, anyway? Would you trust him with a tractor?"

"Sure I would. Better him than a McKieran, but I told you we don't need your field work. Can't you get that through your thick skull?"

"Whoa ..."

Wes gets out of the chair. He leans his hands on the desk and gets his face even with Doug's and Doug just watches him like this is funny, too.

"Cam is smart. He is not a friggin' retard and he never was. He's up at the library every week for another stack of books. Did you know that? When was the last time you read a book, Doug?"

Doug thinks about it a moment. "I read a book about John Diefenbaker. Couple years ago. Good man."

"Yah, your wife got the book and you looked at the first page. Don't BS me, Doug."

"I read it. Most of it."

Wes sits down. "Cam is smarter than the bunch of us put together. Nobody ever saw that. He cooks a damn good pie, too. He cooks just about anything. Better than his gran, even."

"You don't say."

"Someday he's gonna make something of himself."

Wes is thinking of Cam now, at the kitchen table with a book open in front of him. How he gets up to stir something on the stove and then goes right back to the book.

"Why'd they put him in that retarded school anyhow, Wes? Must have been some reason."

"Oh fuck off, you goddamn …"

Wes gets up to leave. He gets to the door and stops. "We got a deal for now. You work Bliss land for another year. End of the season, we talk it over. We squared away?"

"We're square, Wes. Sure we are."

Doug is smirking again and it's all Wes can do not to smash his big baby face.

He goes out and bangs the door behind him.

Pulling the car in by the pump shed, he sees one of his groundhog traps lying by the woodpile. He goes over to pick it up. There's blood all over it and on the ground and flies buzzing around. What the hell …? Then he knows it's not his trap; too much rust on it. It's one of Kyle McKieran's. He leaves the trap where it lies and heads to the house.

Dorie is watching TV. There's a smell like food burning. Cam's banging around in the kitchen. He goes in and Cam's slamming the cupboards — Jesus, he's crying. He looks at Wes with the tears streaming down.

"They wanna take Dorie, Wes. They can take her away legal."

14

CAM IS CRUSHED IN A bear hug now. He starts to feel himself coming back to normal, just from having Wes around.

He tells Wes what happened with the Gurneys and Kyle. He gets back to organizing lunch. He picks up the dishrag still pink with Kyle's blood, rinses it out and wipes all around the sink and drops the rag in the garbage pail.

Cam figures his weird crying was just from everything piling up: the churchies, Kyle, the blood, Dorie running loose in the woods with those traps out, Wes not being here ... And thinking like he did always that Kyle would tell about Gramp, especially now in the hospital, if they give him pills that make him woozy so he says stuff. It was all too much and he started bawling like a little kid. He got some beans heating in a pot but he burned them because he was reading the Children's Aid rules over and over. "Removal from the household," it said. "In the interests of the child."

"Where'd they take Kyle, Cam?"

"Dunno."

"Saw the trap out there when I drove in. Enough blood for a friggin' murder. Anyhow, those old girls can't take Dorie — not them or Children's Aid, either. I'm in legal charge here."

"That's just it. They can take kids legal. Says here. Read it."

Wes glances at the paper.

"Or don't read it, makes no difference."

The phone rings. The hospital wants to speak to Cam. A doctor asks him questions about the trap and what happened. Was Kyle releasing an animal from the trap? What kind? Cam tells him a rabbit, or could be a racoon or a badger, he doesn't know.

"Why don't you just ask Kyle?"

"Kyle is in surgery," says the doctor. "But thank you, you've been a help."

Cam hangs up.

Wes says, "That racoon thing, that's rabies is what they're saying. So they gotta give him the shots just in case. Four big needles in his gut. You get a scratch or anything from that trap?"

Cam takes a good look at his hands, but they look clear.

15

WES FEELS THE SLOW PANIC going though him. Luke Price is standing in the drive, right there in front of him talking, and not looking like a no-good, either. Driving a big Chevy and wearing a white shirt and a tie. Five or six years, at least, since he last saw Luke Price. Dorie wasn't even born likely. Luke's talking about her now. Calling her Dotty. Wes knows for a fact Luke hasn't laid eyes on his daughter since she was a baby, when she came here to Gran and Gramp.

"Her name's Dorie. No one calls her Dotty."

"Well, where is my little darlin', anyways?"

"In the house. Why?"

"How 'bout a smile, Wes? Been a long time. How's the old man — still getting hisself pickled every night?"

"Sam's dead."

"Shit, you mean it?"

"Good as dead. He took off. Not a word from him in months."

Wes can't believe what he just said. He has to be more careful. No goddamn way Luke's coming in to chat with Dorie. He's gotta go.

Cam's out on the porch now. Luke looks over and gets a big fake grin on his face. He starts walking toward the house, the wind flapping his fancy tie over his shoulder.

"Holy …" He calls out, "That you, Cam? I'm Luke, Luke Price. Come to see my little girl."

Wes comes up behind Luke. "You got no right to Dorie."

Luke turns around. He's still smiling. "I'm her family. You folks are the ones with no right. I'm on the straight now, Wes. Working at GM in Oshawa, couple years now."

"Sweeping up?"

"Fuck, no. I'm on the line. Full benefits, better than Stelco. And I got a daughter and the right to see her."

"A bit late. Where you been for five years?"

"C'mon, Wes, can't you be nice?"

"Don't talk nice to me. You know what kinda shape she was in when she came here."

"Blame her mother. Why'd you think I left?"

"Because you didn't care a rat's ass what happened to your own kid. Where's Dorie's mom at now? She still on drugs?"

Luke isn't smiling now. "I don't give a fuck where she is."

Wes watches Luke's eyes flick away, out over the fields, like he might lose his cool. Wes looks him over: his white shirt all fresh starched, tie knotted up tight. Looks like he came straight from church. Except today is Saturday. "You wear that stuffed-shirt getup on the shop floor?"

Luke turns to him. "You gonna ask me in?"

"Why would I friggin' do that?"

"I heard a thing about you, you and Cam … You boys got no business with a kid."

"What the fuck's that mean?"

But Luke's striding toward the house, calling out: "Dotty, your daddy's come to see you! Come on out and let me get a look at you!"

Wes goes after him. He grabs his arm and Luke shakes him off and keeps moving, calling that stupid "Dotty" name like it means something. Wes charges at Luke and takes a flying leap and gets a headlock on him. They go down in the dirt, their legs scrabbling around and Luke throwing punches at Wes's face and mostly missing, until Wes feels his nose crunch. That makes Wes go ape. He's a wild man, he can't even see straight. He's howling and seeing blood and tasting it and he tastes the ground against his face because Luke's on top now, but Wes doesn't let go. His arm's locked in a vise grip on Luke's neck and he's cinching it tighter, tighter. Even tighter. Cam is shouting at him. Then Luke's body goes soft.

"Wes, let him go. Jesus. Let him go!"

"He's faking."

"I don't think so."

Wes lets his grip relax. He gets untangled from Luke and staggers up. His nose is pouring blood. Luke is motionless, lying twisted on his side with his head thrown back, Wes's blood all over his white shirt. Wes stands there with the blood still coming, running into his mouth. Luke still isn't moving. Wes winds up and nails him with a boot square in the nuts. Then he gets in a few hard kicks to his stomach before Cam pulls him away.

"Jeez, Wes, aw jeez … Go in the house, will you."

"Fucker. I'll kill him."

"Go!"

Dorie's watching from the window upstairs. She heard the noise. She looked and she saw them fighting. Wes is bleeding from his face now. The other man is on the ground. Wes comes in the house but Cam stays out there. He shakes the man's shoulder but the man just flops over on his back and lies still. Cam looks at him for a long time and then Wes comes out and they start arguing. Cam looks real upset. They come back inside but they don't stop shouting.

But now the man on the ground is moving. His whole body is shaking. Stuff comes out his mouth. It's a little bit and then it's a whole lot. It bubbles up and goes down the side of his face and on the ground. His chest is going up and down. Cam and Wes are still yelling. Dorie goes into the bathroom. She sits in the tub and hums and tries to ignore the noise downstairs. After a while, things are quiet.

Later, Cam comes upstairs. He's acting strange. He takes off his pants and puts on a clean pair. He says he's going out with Wes. They won't be gone too long.

"Why was Wes fighting?"

"Just some crazy fella. He's drunk, Dor, he's so drunk he can't even move. He sicked up all over. We gotta drive him home."

"How'd he drive here?"

"Dunno. He could've crashed."

"Why'd he come see Wes?"

"Told you. He's crazy."

Cam pitches his puke-stained jeans down the cellar stairs on his way out. Wes is waiting in Luke's car. Cam gets behind the wheel of Wes's Ford and they drive out to the road, Cam following behind the Chev. Cam is shaking. He's crying, tears squeezing out of his eyes from panic and crazy thoughts. Because they got a dead man there, up there in the car with Wes. He still can't believe it.

Luke's face was blue. Cam shook him and put his ear against his chest, but there was nothing, no sound at all. It made him remember Gramp that morning he found him on the sofa. Nothing but a sack of bones and dead human flesh.

They drive to the bushy land west of Cargill. There's some dirt tracks through the woods there that dead-end at the marshy spots. Wes rigs Luke's car to rev fast then reaches in the window and drops the shift into drive. The car heads straight into the marsh and stops dead with its front sunk in the mucky water and the rear end tipped up. They stand there watching the wheels spin a while until the engine chokes and dies.

Luke's still laid out in the back seat. They argue a bit about putting him in the trunk, or maybe in the driver's seat so it looks more normal. Then they just leave him. They figure it'll be weeks or more before anyone finds him.

16

TWO DAYS LATER, CAM AND Wes have a giant fight in the kitchen, early, before the sun is even up. Neither of them slept for two nights. Cam is so mad at Wes he can't think, he can't do anything but shout and break stuff. He already broke plates and a chair and he can't stop yelling how much shit they're in because of Wes. Then Wes stops shouting back. He sits bent over, staring at the floor with his hands wrapped behind the back of his head.

The yelling is finished. The house is quiet but Cam's head is ringing. Wes is sitting there, kind of rocking. Cam goes out to the porch. Looking at the dark fields and the sky getting pink in the east, he starts to feel his normal self coming back. He cries a little, but he stops it and goes back to the kitchen. Wes is still in the chair, hunched over.

"Wes." His voice comes out hoarse. "I didn't mean that stuff."

Wes hardly moves. Just shakes his head a little. Cam stares around the kitchen at the smashed pieces of plate and the splintered chair. He starts to pick up the broken crockery. He puts the broken chair upright and it sits there on three legs. He and Wes both stare at it. Wes reaches out and gives it a little tap and it falls over.

Cam says, "Gramp had some wood glue, didn't he?"

"Cellar. I'll get it."

"Think there's some clamps too, Wes."

"Yup."

Cam goes upstairs to see about Dorie. She's still in bed but she's not sleeping. She asks why they were fighting so bad and Cam tells her it's about that drunken idiot that came by. Cam sits on the bed with her.

"Wes knows him, Dor. I guess from Stelco. He just came round here to make trouble and Wes got out of control kind of. I was mad at Wes for beating up on the guy and I got even madder this morning. But we're all patched up now."

✽

Next morning when they're eating breakfast, Dorie says, "I wanna go to the lie berry."

"The library? Why you wanna go there?"

"You can take me. It can be like school."

"Think you're ready for school?"

"Umm, you can help me read. I'm sick of this dump."

"What?"

"I'm sick to death of it." She's talking fancy like a TV actress.

Cam stares at her. "Whatta you mean 'dump'? We've got a real decent life here. Don't say that again, Dor."

Wes says, "Listen, Dor, you say that to the church ladies and they'll take you out of here and put you in some stranger's place. Don't ever bad-talk your own home or your own family."

"You're not my own family."

Wes and Cam look at each other. Cam says, "Of course we are. Same as your mum and dad that are gone, except we love you, Dor. They never did, not really."

"Can we go to the Hanover Fair?"

"Well, I guess we can. What you think, Wes?"

"Dunno. I gotta think about it."

Cam's thinking, too. He's thinking it's what families do. They play the carnival games and go on the rides. He's been on a ride maybe only twice in his life. And there's hot dogs and candy floss and all that. And baking contests.

"It's a family thing, right, Wes? We oughta do that. Be a family. Like regular folks."

"Regular? That's a funny one."

"See, we gotta show them we're normal."

Wes laughs. He keeps laughing until he's wiping tears away. When he stops, he's staring with his eyes wide. He gets up.

"I'm going next door. See if they know anything."

"You can't ask them that."

"Ask them what, what am I gonna ask them? 'You folks see us dragging that dead fella into the car the other day?' Frig, Cam. I got a brain, okay?"

Wes goes out. Cam wants to strangle him.

The screen door slams and Dorie says, "Why did Wes say a 'dead fella'?"

"It was a joke."

Dorie is quiet for a long time, then she says, "You said Wes killed him. You said it when you were fighting. I heard."

"I was upset. I was wrong. The guy had a heart attack or, frig, I dunno what, he got sick. Nobody killed anybody."

"Did you take him to the doctor?"

"Yes. To the hospital. Listen, let's go to the library this aft. We'll find some really swell books that you can read. I'll help you read them."

"Is the sick man my daddy?"

"Jeez. No. He's not your daddy. Why would you ..."

Cam gets out of his chair and starts cleaning up the breakfast things. He's real jittery and Dorie's watching him with her head leaning the way it does when she doesn't believe him, the BS he tells her. But you've got to BS kids about some things, the bad things, about the shit of the world.

"Anyways, Dor, your daddy was just mean to you all the time and then he took off, he left you all alone. You know that, right?"

"Yip." But she's still leaning her head over.

✿

Turns out there's no one at the McKierans'. Wes is keeping one eye out the kitchen window for Kate's car and another one for anyone coming up from the barn, but the place feels deserted. The sink and the drainboard are dry as a bone. A cup on the table has a skin of dried coffee at the bottom.

He's snooping, not even knowing what he's looking for. He just knows he might find something, something he could use against these people. Kate McKieran and her dumb-ass sons are the cause of most every crap thing that's happened since Gramp died.

So he's going around opening cupboards and drawers but he's careful not to put anything out of place when he pokes around. There's a jar in behind the cereal boxes with some change and a couple dollar bills in it. There's a shelf of Heinz soup and Chef Boyardee and the tinned corned beef with the steer's head on the label. Wes's mum used to open a tin of that and heat it up with ketchup and canned corn.

In a drawer he finds some personal bank cheques: Mr. and Mrs. Lloyd McKieran, RR#3, Lucknow, Ont. There's a man's wallet with the leather warped and shiny from years in a pocket. The old stuff that widows keep. Kate has had her troubles. But she's still a nutcase Bible-thumper.

Wes looks in the sitting room where the TV is — was. The set is gone. Maybe sold or repossessed. He scans out the windows. It's just barely eight in the morning, not much chance they'd be coming in from away. He goes upstairs. In Kate's room the bed is made, but the boys' rooms have mussed-up sheets and clothes scattered around. He puts his head in the bathroom. Christ, there's turds floating in the toilet. Gotta be Kyle's or Tom's. Ma would flush.

He's not interested in Kate's room but he goes in to snoop the boys'. He figures Kyle's is the one with a couple rabbit feet hanging on a piece of twine. The room has a sweaty smell. Comic books are lying around, *Superman* and *Green Hornet*, some Bible comics.

Wes stands in the musty heat and looks around. There's a pile of clothes by the bed: crumpled socks, T-shirts, stained jockey shorts. Mom is letting things go, by the look of it. He stops at the door to Kate's room. She's got a framed picture of Jesus on her dresser. Rays of light are coming out his eyes onto a praying girl and boy.

Wes goes back down to the kitchen. He takes a look in the fridge. There's a headless skinned rabbit on a piece of newspaper, the raw meat puckered and dried out. He thuds the door shut.

By the phone, Wes sees a notepad. Someone's written a number on it: *49183-H.*

Right away Wes knows it's an Ontario licence plate number. Then in his mind he sees the "H" on the back end of Luke Price's Chevy. He tears off the note and pockets it. On the way out he puts the house key back in its hiding spot on top of the door frame. Stupid. Why do folks do that?

And now he's on the road heading to the woods past Cargill. He didn't say a word to Cam when he came back for his car. Why even start about it? He can deal with this on his own.

It takes him two tries to find the right track winding toward the marshland, but now he's on the one that jogs his memory — the curves and dips, the tree branches slapping the windshield at the narrow parts. Wes is not sure what he'll do when he gets there. He's hoping the plate number won't match. If it does, then what? Christ. He'll go on instinct.

The trees give way to the lumpy, scrubby land around the marsh. There's the car, the ass end tipped up so he's looking at the rear axle. The front must've sunk deeper in the muck. And there's the "H" on the plate. Wes stops the car and sits staring at the plate number. He digs the pencilled note out of his pocket. The number's an exact match. He doesn't get out of his car. One thing keeping him there is the smell. It has to be from the Chevy. Three days now in August sun.

He stares at the note. Wouldn't be the boys writing down a plate number. Kyle likely can't write at all these days. Kate'd be the one to keep track that way, watch who's coming and going. How did she see a car plate so clear from her house? This is what's been banging around inside Wes's head all the way out here. What did Kate or the boys see or not see? Thinking on it makes Wes's heart race. The idea that they saw him and Cam dragging Luke to the car, and blood all over.

"There's no friggin' way," Wes says out loud. Anywhere close enough for her to see the plate and they would've seen her there. She'd have to be right in their lane coming up from the road. But, fuck, none of it matters. He's got to assume the worst. Which is: she can't know that Luke is dead, but she might know that he was messed up bad and they tossed him in the back seat and drove away with him.

Wes feels like he could have a stroke or something if he doesn't get hold of himself. He says out loud to himself to stay calm, just look at it calm and rational. To start with, he's gotta take those plates off. He forces himself out of the car.

He stands there in the dead-dog stink. He runs through in his mind what he has to do. He goes and opens his trunk and gets out his tool kit. He's got some clean rags and he finds one that'll work for a mask over his nose and mouth. How in hell will he get the front plate off? Maybe it's not too far submerged. Or maybe he'll be up to his eyeballs in swamp mud. Well, fuck, here we go.

The back plate comes off easy with his lock-wrench. He comes round the side of the Chev and glances inside. Luke's bloated up. His stomach's swelled, his face all puffed out. He's greeny-purple coloured. Lots of flies on him and buzzing around the open windows. The rag mask is not helping at all. The stench sticks in Wes's throat.

Okay, into the swamp. Right away he's up to his waist, dragging his feet out of sucking mud to get round the front and reach down for the plate. It's a couple feet under in the churned-up slurry of muck. He can get the bolts off by feel. The black water grazes his chin and soaks up into his mask, suffocating him. He finally tears it off.

He needs the ownership and insurance cards. He reaches into the front window and pops the glovebox. There they are, right on top in a plastic folder. He catches sight of Luke's address, an apartment in Scarborough. For the first time Wes wonders if there's someone waiting for Luke to come home. He shoves the idea to the back of his mind.

He has left Luke's wallet for last. He moves away from the car, takes some deep breaths and holds a big one. He goes and opens the back door. He sees a bulge, thank God, in Luke's side pants pocket. He won't need to roll him over. He sticks his fingers in the pocket slit. The corpse bloat makes it so tight he can hardly force his hand in. Jesus, here come the heaves. He gets his hand on the wallet and yanks it out as the vomit spews from him.

He goes back to his car and chucks all the evidence in the trunk. He'll burn and bury it at home. He walks twenty or thirty yards back from the car and lies down in the weeds. He thinks he could die right here and now and not care except for Cam's sake. And Dorie. He can smell the normal woods smell here, the vegetation and the damp earth. He breathes it in. He still has to find the vehicle serial number on the engine block and file or chisel it till it's unreadable.

Back out near the main road, Wes passes a stack of old cedar rails. He stops and drags a few rails out to block the track, then keeps on with the rest of them until he's got a roadblock about waist high. On the highway, he feels almost relieved. He tells himself it'll be weeks or months before anyone finds Luke. It'll be in the news. Maybe even a picture of the car. Just another dark-blue Chevy Impala. There's a fair number of those. How did Kate see the friggin' plate number? It makes no sense. Even if she was staring out her window or out in her yard, the car would've been hidden behind the windbreak.

What's he gonna tell Cam? He's got mud from his neck down. He smells like swamp and human decay. He'll have to explain everything, no other way. He'll hold off until he has a proper wash-up and fresh clothes. He'll get himself a beer and they'll take a walk, out where Dorie can't hear a word.

They're sitting on the porch. It's dusk and Dorie's asleep on the daybed. Wes has told Cam the whole story. They've talked it all through until there's no more talk in them. Wes is so beat he can hardly move. But his mind is still there at the swamp. He still smells it. Wes did the best he could to fix things — Cam knows that and he said so. When they went out to the north field to talk, Cam was listening to the part about Luke and the Chevy just staring with his mouth open. He was what you call speechless.

Wes has already had three beers, something he does once a year at most. Cam says he'll get another one if Wes wants it. Wes thinks a bit and says no. They sit looking out at the first stars. The air is clear and warm, dry like September.

Cam says, "Know what, Wes? I'm thinking Luke Price went in the wrong drive, looking for us. He knocked at the McKierans' and she set him right, and being such a nosy parker she wrote down his plate number. So that's all she's got on us. And she doesn't even have that because you took the number."

"Jesus."

"Just logical."

"That's it. You got a head for that."

"Maybe. But I could never do what you did today, Wes. Not a chance."

"Should've done it on the first run."

❖

A couple days later, Wes is out front doing some mowing and he sees Kate's rusted-out station wagon turn into her drive. He can't help himself. He's got to know what's up, what her connection is with Luke Price's Chevy. He asks Cam to make a pie so he can take it over and pass on their best wishes for Kyle's recovery from his wounds. Wes honestly feels kind of bad for the boy. What are the chances? A lightning bolt knocks out one arm and a rusty trap gets the other one. But if you're a McKieran, it seems the odds are pretty high for accidents.

Wes has to go get ingredients for Cam, even the apples this time — their own are mostly on the ground now. He does a quick run into Walkerton and comes home with a bushel of Macs. He could eat four or five of those a day aside from pies. When he comes in with them, Cam's just getting dinner started.

He stares at the heaping bushel. "How much pie you think we can eat, Wes?"

"Much as you can make."

"You wanna make our supper, then?"

"Don't get sore."

"Who's sore?"

They watch each other a moment. Wes moves close to Cam and presses him gently against the wall by the Moffat.

"I got a pot boiling there." Cam nods at the stove.

Wes reaches over and shuts off the burner.

Dorie doesn't even glance at them when they go past the sitting room and upstairs. They don't ever use the room that Cam and Dorie share, only Wes's room.

Wes closes the door and then their hands are all over. They don't kiss because Cam doesn't like it, not on the lips. But anywhere else is just fine.

When they're done, they lie there hearing *Rocky and Bullwinkle* come up through the floor grate in the hall. It's a just-before-suppertime sound.

"I gotta get the potatoes going."

"Cam."

"Yup?"

"We got to do something. Some thinking. About our ..."

"Our ..."

"Situation."

Cam's pulling on his jeans now. Wes waits for him to say something, but he doesn't. Cam grabs his T-shirt off the floor and puts it on and just stands there with his back to Wes. "You mean about what we just ..."

"Frig, no, not that. About Kyle and burning Gramp, and Dorie and Children's Aid."

"That's two situations right there, Wes. Add Luke Price and we got three."

Cam goes out and clomps down the stairs.

Wes lies on the bed with his mind kind of blanked out, like there's too much for his brain to even get a start on. The late sun is on the wall beside him, coming in low through the maples. The room has a dry-summer-heat smell, mixed right now with the smell of spunk. Wes isn't thinking about anything. All he can do is feel full up with love and hurt for Cam. It's like a pain and the best thing ever, all twisted together inside him. He lies there a long time watching the leaf shadows moving on the wall.

17

WES GOES OVER WITH A fresh pie about noon next day. The day is 100 percent September even though it's still August. Not a cloud anywhere, warm enough for just a T-shirt, but the air is clear and dry, not muggy at all. He almost has a spring in his step as he walks the dusty shoulder over to the McKierans' drive. He knows it's really the weather and the warm apple pie scent that's doing this to him — sure as hell isn't the chat he's about to have with Kate.

He knocks politely on the screen door.

"Hellooo … Kate? It's Wes Cody."

Tom comes round the corner from the sitting room. "My mom's out the back."

"How's your brother doing, Tom?"

"Back in hospital. He's infected."

"Sorry to hear that. Can I come in? Brought you folks a pie."

Wes comes through to the kitchen. There's a stack of unhusked corn on the table. Maybe from their field, but Wes'll just ignore that. Tom takes the pie from him and stares at it without so much as a smile or a thank you. He puts it beside the corn and stands there like a sad puppy.

"Maybe you can take some of that for Kyle."

"He's not eating much."

Wes sees the top of Kate's head go by the kitchen window. Then she's up the steps and in the back door with the screen slapping shut behind her. She looks Wes up and down, kind of vibrating.

"You've got a nerve. Think you can just waltz in here?"

"Thought I'd see how Kyle's doing, is all."

"Tom, go outside."

Tom heads out the door.

Kate looks ready to spit on Wes. "You people ..."

"What?"

"Stay away from my boys."

"You tell your boys to stay away from Dorie. And keep their damn traps out of our woods."

"Your girl was there with him when he got hurt."

"What, it's her fault? It's a miracle Dorie didn't get herself hurt by Kyle's traps. On our friggin' land."

"Get out of my house."

"It's just dumb luck Kyle didn't take his own hand off months ago. Where is the boy's brain? Where was his mother when he went out spreading manure in a lightning storm?"

"Out! Get out!"

Wes doesn't back off. He actually moves closer to her. "Your boy is a deviant. What else do you call it when he takes a little girl in the barn for his perversions? You let him anywhere near our Dorie again and —"

"She's not your Dorie. Her father came here looking for her. I hope he gets her and I told him so, too."

"He won't. Not a chance in hell."

Kate gets right up in Wes's face. "You know what hell is? Do you have any idea? You might find out. What kind of a teenage boy bakes pies and cooks meals? He's a dandy little wife to you, isn't he. No wonder that girl is — my Lord, you people are sick."

Wes is knocked for a loop by this. He's really rattled. He's never hit a woman and now he's feeling an inch away from doing it. Instead he grabs the pie off the table and rams it against the nearest thing to Kate, which is the fridge. She lets out a little sound, not even a scream. They stare at apple chunks and pastry sliding down the fridge door.

Wes goes by Tom partway down the drive. When he's hardly past him, the boy says something, just one word. Wes keeps walking. He gets to the road and turns east, toward town.

He's ready for a cold beer after his walk in the sun. Christ, when was the last time he walked to town? Ever? He's got a fiver and some change in his wallet. Enough for a couple beers and a sandwich at the Bruce.

He phones Cam from the booth in the hotel lobby, says he just dropped down the road to Sproule's where he takes the Ford for work, and Bud's got him talking. Stupid lie, and then he's telling other lies about his chat with Kate. He makes it sound all right for Cam, except for Kyle being back in hospital and Kate talking her usual Bible crap. But it's not all right and he just can't go home right now. He needs to think in peace without Cam there to get fussed and himself all knotted up inside.

In the beverage room, he sits at a table away from the windows. Wes's dad used to come in here Saturday afternoons. Sometimes he'd bring Wes along and Wes would sit in the lobby and watch the people coming and going. He could see his dad through the doors to the barroom, drinking draft beers with his buddies. If he caught Wes looking at him, he'd wink. He always gave Wes enough money to buy something from the candy machine.

Dumb memories. What's he doing here, anyway? He's feeling not like himself, like he's watching things happening to him and it makes no sense, even though everything in here still looks pretty much exactly the way it did when he was eight or ten years old. Same tables, same beer glasses, same pickled eggs in the big jar.

They never did offer Black Horse in here. Wes makes do with Labatt 50 from the keg. He orders a grilled cheese and bacon so he's not looking like some idler who drinks at noon. There's already near a dozen at the tables. Three old codgers by the front window look like they might just about live here. Christ, he hopes he's never like them.

"Queers." That's the word Tom said in the drive. He's sure of it. And where would he learn that word but from his mother. Or could be from TV. When Wes thinks about queers, it's Lorne Gibbs and Jerry Parsons, fairy types in school who threw baseballs like a girl. Lorne and Jerry were in the drama club at Walkerton Collegiate. Jerry had a singing part in *Oklahoma!* He even sang kind of girly. Not much like a cowboy, anyway.

Wes was sporty in school, not football and such, but gymnastics and track. He was a sprinter, even won a prize once at intercollegiate. But he didn't make fun of fairies, not like the football players did. Wes was no fairy, but he liked looking at boys. He always did, right from the time he was little.

The beer helps him relax and not think too negative about their situation, or like Cam said, their situations. Things just snowballed. Add to that some rotten bad luck. And then Wes let his temper get the better of him with Luke. He has never in his life wanted to actually kill someone — except maybe Gramp. Luke Price was an accident. He must've had heart failure or something. Wes has been lying awake at night thinking how unfair it is. A two-minute fight ends up with this horrible thing. Now they have to hope Luke sits out there long enough so there's nothing left to identify.

The Gurney sisters are probably thinking the queer bullshit, too. He can picture them clucking about all the sinners of this world. Kate McKieran, too, just because a boy is making pies and because she's got herself all twisted about the sex perversion of her lily-white sons — like a kid Dorie's age can actually turn a teenager into a pervert? Christ almighty. It's Kate and the Gurneys who're the perverts. That's it. They point the finger, but it's them.

Wes stares into his beer. He looks around the barroom. A bunch of sad oldies letting themselves rot in a rundown hotel bar, but they'd sure as hell know what to think about queers. People have no idea. All they see is their own dumb-ass ideas about normal and decent. What he feels about Cam is a thing they will never understand. So people can go fuck themselves.

Wes picks up his grilled cheese and chomps into it. He finishes it off like he's tearing Kate McKieran limb from limb with his teeth. An old guy across the room is staring at him like he's some kind of zoo animal. He probably looks it.

He spends the last of his cash on another beer and when it's gone, he sits for a long time with his mind turning over and over until it stalls. Then he realizes he better get home to Cam. So he gets out of his chair and walks a straight line to the barman and pays his tab.

Out heading west past the fields, he's thinking he won't tell Cam about the queer stuff. There's nothing to talk about because that's not what they are. And no one can ever prove it.

18

"WES, WE GOTTA BURY HIM. Now. Today."

Cam's been up half the night with worry. He came down before dawn and poured a bowl of cereal and it sat getting soggy while his mind went over and over the same thing. It's in the police shows and *Perry Mason*: dental records. All they need to be sure they found Luke Price is his teeth, and they have even more than that. They got teeth and his car and his clothes and whatever else Wes forgot to look for. They need to get Luke out of the car and bury him far away somewhere. No choice.

So when Wes came downstairs, Cam told him. Now Wes is pacing around the kitchen.

"Wes?"

Wes stops and stares at him. He says, "I gotta think," and he goes out through the porch and up toward the barn. After a few minutes, Cam heads out after him. Wes is in the barn, staring at the old trailer that Gramp built from wood planks and a truck axle. Cam can barely remember it being anyplace except right here in the back of the barn with flat tires and piled with old tools and junk.

Wes starts taking the junk off it. "You gonna help me or just stand there?"

They get it cleared off and Wes goes out to his car and gets his jack and lug wrench. He sweats and strains until he gets the wheels off the trailer, then he backs his car into the barn and throws the wheels into the trunk. He examines the cracked rubber on the tires before he chucks the lid shut.

"Let's hope they hold air."

Wes comes back with the pumped-up tires, a roll of heavy black plastic like he wrapped Gramp with, a coil of rope and two pairs of rubber work gloves. They go get changed into their oldest clothes. Dorie's watching them out one eye and *Romper Room* out the other. For sure she heard them talking this morning. Cam tells her they got to do some work hauling stuff for the Johnstones, then he makes her a Cheez Whiz and relish sandwich and wraps it up and tells her she has to wait till lunchtime for it.

They're driving about twenty-five miles an hour because the trailer fishtails all over if they do highway speed. Gramp made the trailer for hitching to a pickup. The hitch on Wes's car is about a foot lower, so the trailer's at a crazy angle with its tail stuck up in the air. Wes looped a chain from his bumper to make it more secure and now he's fighting the steering wheel and throwing nervous looks in the rear-view. They're not saying much, just a word now and then, never about Luke Price. Cam wonders what the plan is. Maybe Wes doesn't have one.

Past Cargill, they turn onto the winding dirt track through the trees. Cam feels the fear sweat dripping from his armpits. He can smell it coming from himself and from Wes, too. They go a little ways in and there's a stack of fence rails blocking them.

"We got the wrong road, Wes."

"Nope. Gimme a hand."

They clear the way and keep going in. Cam's getting the shakes now.

"Jeez, this is crazy. Where we gonna take him?"

Wes says right away, "Gravel pit, out by Chepstow." He has a hard look on his face, like he's making himself strong.

The trees thin out to a grassy stretch. Cam sees the back end of Luke's car, nose down in the swamp.

"What's that smell?"

"Whadda you think?"

"The swamp?"

Wes laughs, but like a bark. "Jesus, don't you remember Gramp in the cold room?"

"Doesn't smell like that."

"Well, see, if you think about it two friggin' seconds, Gramp wasn't in a car in the hot sun. He rotted slow."

"Stop the car a minute. Wes? STOP THE CAR."

Wes jams on the brakes. They sit there staring at the Chevy. The only sound is flies zooming by.

Cam says, "We don't have to bury him. We blow up the gas tank, burn him like Gramp."

"Teeth don't burn. Gotta be buried."

They sit thinking about that.

Wes says, "Okay, blow up the car. But first we get Luke out."

"Frig, let's just do it."

Wes drives up close and stops. Clouds of flies are all around the Chev. The smell is horrible. It's in Cam's nose and throat, hanging thick in the air all around them. Then he remembers the dead pig he found once, out on the concession road, seething with maggots like it was alive.

"Gonna puke, Wes."

"Do it now. And start breathing through your mouth."

Cam gets out of the car and barfs into the weeds. Meanwhile Wes is manoeuvring the Ford over the lumpy ground. He gets backed up to the side of Luke's car. The tipped-up trailer is too high. Wes unhitches the trailer and tips it the other way so the tailgate rests on the ground near the Chev's back door.

They get gloved up and they stand there with flies buzzing in their faces, looking at this bloated thing that is Luke Price. Cam looks, then doesn't look. Then he looks again. Luke's head is closest. His decayed face is there, greeny-purple with white worms crawling in his eyes and mouth. His nose and lips are gone. His mouth is just a hole with teeth smiling. Like he loves chewing maggots. His body is gigantic. The shirt buttons are popped and his belly looks like it could burst.

Wes gets one foot in on the floor of the back seat and reaches in with an end of rope. He shifts Luke's arms and loops the rope around under both armpits. The smell gets worse. It's burning Cam's eyes and clogging the back of his throat so he feels like he might suffocate. He moves away and takes some breaths. Wes is swearing the whole time. His face is turning red. He knots the rope and backs fast away from the car.

They get the bolt of black plastic from the trunk and roll it out flat on the bed of the trailer. Wes cuts it long so he can run it right across the tailgate and under the Chev.

"Don't wanna leave any of him on the ground here."

They brace themselves in the trailer and start pulling on the rope. Luke's head drops off the car seat and bumps onto the door frame. Worms drop off him and squirm on the black plastic. They drag him slowly out of the car. When he's half out, his legs flop sideways and one of his feet jams under the front seat. They pull harder. The rope is cutting into his armpits and making corpse-ooze soak out into his shirt. Maggots come crawling out of his clothes. They yank until his foot pops free and they fall backward and slide down the plastic sheeting. They're scrambling to get up, but the plastic is too slippery. Their feet are kicking Luke. They finally pull themselves over the sides of the trailer. Cam ends up in swamp water up to his knees.

Wes is saying "Jesus Christ almighty" and worse things over and over. He takes hold of the rope and goes round between the trailer and the Ford. Cam joins him and they haul on the rope until Luke is slid up into the trailer. Wes cuts another length of plastic. They cover the body with it and nail it tight to the planks of the trailer bed.

They have to leave without burning the Chevy — no matches. Instead they go through the car and take anything with any connection to Luke. Wes finds repair receipts and other things he missed the first time.

On the highway, they're both quiet. It's sinking in for Cam that they actually have Dorie's real dad there in the back. Maybe he could've been an okay father, with his job at GM and his shirt and tie and a decent car too. Maybe he wasn't a no-good anymore. But he used to be. That's why Dorie came to the Blisses. And that's why Luke is dead.

Cam watches the fields and side roads going past at twenty-five miles an hour. "How far's Chepstow, Wes?"

"Close now."

"How come a gravel pit? Don't people go there to get gravel?"

"Out of business now, ten years at least."

"But folks need gravel, right?"

Wes looks at him. "You got a better idea?"

"Well, sure. Maybe someplace folks don't go. Ever."

Wes drives, staring straight ahead.

Cam says, "Like our marsh. We burn Luke and put him in the marsh with Gramp and that's it. We're done."

Wes keeps driving but Cam can see him thinking. They come to Chepstow. Just past the "Welcome" sign, Wes pulls into a filling station. He rolls past the pumps to U-turn out the other side.

There's a couple boys sitting on the back end of a pickup. While Wes is waiting to turn back eastbound, one of them says, "Crikey, what you hauling there, dead cow? Peee-yewww!" They're still carrying on when Wes pulls out.

Wes stops talking. If Cam asks him anything, he hardly seems to hear, or he just grunts. Cam looks at his face and the sweat beading up on his forehead and running down and his eyes wide staring ahead at the road, but he knows Wes is not staring at the road at all. Wes's mind is somewhere else, somewhere awful. He's looking into a hell pit.

They're partway home and Wes cranks the wheel sudden into the BP station outside Mildmay. The tires spray gravel and the trailer almost misses the entrance, one tire jolting on the cement curb. He pulls over to the edge of the lot and brakes hard to a stop.

"Jesus, Wes …"

"Shuddup." Wes glares at him. Then he closes his eyes, like he's trying to get a grip.

"You gotta calm down."

"Ha. That's … Ha. Okay, then. You calm down. Go ahead."

"All right, I will. One of us gotta. Why'd you stop here?"

"Gas. GAS. And we buy a couple extra cans."

"We got two gas cans in the trunk, Wes."

"We're getting two more. And don't talk back to me. DON'T EVEN FUCKING TRY. Now get out and go check the friggin' cargo."

Wes looks like his face might catch on fire, he's so red. Cam gets out. His legs feel like rubber but he concentrates on acting normal, like he's bored with this boring trip, having to drive a dead cow to the incinerator. He walks around making sure the plastic sheet is holding down okay. He tries not to breathe through his nose. It's not so bad on the one side of the trailer because there's a steady wind blowing, actually blowing the smell away from the filling station. So they got lucky with that. They'll be needing a lot more luck is what Cam's thinking.

Wes is inside the station now. A beat-up truck is just pulling in at the pumps. An old guy in overalls climbs out of the cab and lights a smoke and moves off a little bit while the gas jockey fills her up. He stares a long time over at Cam. Then he starts walking toward him.

"Well, lookit that." The old guy keeps coming until he's close by Cam. "I think I seen this trailer before."

"Not much chance of that. Been in our barn ten years, anyways."

"Could be, but I seen it when it was new made. Sam Bliss built this thing. You Cam?"

"Um, yessir."

"All growed up. You in regular school now?"

"No, sir. Gramp took me out."

"I traded him that old truck axle for a load of feed corn. Whew! What in hell you got there?"

"Cow. I mean a calf."

"Jesus. Why'nt you just bury it?"

"Law says you gotta incinerate."

"You pullin' my leg? Heck, boy, dig a hole. How's your grampa these days?"

"He's gone."

"Whatcha mean gone?"

"Went away. We got Wes now."

Then Wes is calling to Cam. He's at the pumps with two shiny red gas cans. He says to get the other two cans from the trunk and bring them over. Cam does what he's told. The old guy is watching all this, then he starts staring at the black plastic, really giving it a look over. He's still standing there when Cam and Wes come back with the filled cans and heft them into the trunk.

"You must be Wes."

"That's about right."

"Ted Wrigley. I knew Sam. Took off, did he?"

"Yup, he did." Wes chucks the trunk lid shut and keeps moving. "Cam, get in the car. Nice to meet you, Ted."

"Where you gonna incinerate that thing?"

Cam says, "Usual place."

"Neustadt? They closed that down. Got it in Harriston now."

"Yah," says Wes, "we know."

"Bit of a trek down there."

"Let's go, Cam."

They get in the car. Ted Wrigley stares at them the whole time until they're turned back on the highway. Cam's thinking they should've turned left, toward Harriston, just to show Ted. But he's afraid to say anything.

Dorie thinks about her cheese sandwich wrapped in wax paper in the kitchen. She could have it anytime and Cam won't ever know, so she takes it and goes to the sofa to eat and watch TV. She can't have Cheezies today because Cam put the bag in the high-up cupboard. She watches cartoons awhile and then there's nothing on but boring grown-up shows.

Cam and Wes lied to her. They didn't really go hauling stuff. When they come back, she'll ask them, *How come you can lie and I'm never supposed to?* They were talking about hauling a dead person. It's the man Wes fought with and Cam said was sick, but he's really dead.

Dorie falls asleep awhile. When she wakes up, *Bugs Bunny* is on and she wishes everything was Cheezies so she could have some. She can see in her head where Cam put them at the very top, over the fridge.

She goes into the kitchen. The cupboard door is open a bit and she sees the orange cellophane bag there. She drags a chair over and climbs up so she's standing on the drainboard and she can lean overtop the fridge, but her arm's not long enough. But she could use something. Maybe the wooden spoon in the dish rack. It works!

When she's back at the TV, someone starts knocking.

"Anyone there? Hello?"

Sounds like a boy. Not Kyle, though — maybe his little brother. Dorie goes and peeks around the corner. She sees Tom McKieran though the screen. She pulls back her head quick.

"Who's that there? I come for Kyle's rabbit trap."

Dorie stands quiet and waits.

"Hey, I seen you, okay? It's Tom."

Dorie says, "No one's here."

"Just gimme the trap."

"Don't got it."

When Dorie goes back to the sofa, she hears the screen door open. Tom comes into the sitting room. Dorie just watches the TV like he's not there.

"Where your folks gone?"

"Nowhere."

Dorie stares at the TV. Tom comes and sits at the other end of the sofa. They watch a Road Runner cartoon. Tom laughs sometimes.

"Let me have a Cheezie?"

"NO."

"Jeepers, okay."

Dorie looks at Tom. His face is real red. "You got a sunburn."

"Nope, that's from the lightning."

"You shoulda stayed outta the field."

"Shut up."

"Why?"

Tom looks at her a long time. "Why're you wearing just underpants?"

"GO AWAY — I'M TELLING WES."

"Okay, then, where's the trap?"

"You're gonna get heck if you don't go away."

"I'm looking in your barn. It's our trap and I got the right."

They stop in the drive so Wes can get some matches before they drive Luke down to the burning place. Cam goes to check on Dorie. He sees the bag of Cheezies and right away he's yelling at her. He grabs the bag and spills them all over and he yanks Dorie's arm and drags her off the sofa.

"WHY'RE YOU SO BAD ALWAYS? WHY? GO UPSTAIRS AND WASH YOUR DIRTY FACE."

Dorie goes upstairs. At the top, she shouts down how mean Cam is. She's crying. He knows he must've hurt her arm. But it's her own fault for disobeying.

He goes out onto the porch. Wes is coming across the yard with Tom McKieran. He's got Tom by the scruff of the neck, shoving him along. Tom pulls away from him and heads down the drive. He stops by the Ford and starts shouting about Kyle and the rabbit trap and how Kyle's still in hospital and it's all their fault. Then he turns and stares at the hump of plastic that's Luke.

"Ew, what's that stink?"

Wes says, "Get off our land, Tom. And stay away, you and Kyle both, or I'll get the OPP on you."

They get Luke down by the marsh and unloaded onto the ground. He smells worse than ever from stewing under the plastic. They gather some dry branches out of the windbreak and pile them around the body, then soak it all with four cans of gasoline.

19

DORIE CAN SEE THE SMOKE coming up. It's just like Gramp burning. But it's Luke Price. They lied but she knows. She saw the trailer. They drove down there with him.

Someone's knocking. It better not be Tom again. Dorie looks and she nearly pees herself. It's a church lady! Dorie shouts that Cam and Wes went out.

"I'll come in, then, Dorie, might I? I have some good news. I'll come in now and we can have a chat. Would that be all right?"

The voice is sweet as pie but it's fake. The screen door opens and then the lady is right there with Dorie in the sitting room. She's the fat one.

"They left you alone here, did they? Well, that's just a crime. May I sit with you? Come on now, come sit beside me and I'll tell you a secret."

The lady plops her bum down on the sofa like she's all set for fun.

Dorie won't look at her. "You smell."

"I what?"

"SMELL."

The lady stares at her. "Do you know what, Dorie? You smell too. You smell dirty, like you need to wash. And that's only one thing you need that you don't get in this house, just a proper bath. Aside from all the other things."

"I hate baths. I really hate them."

"We can change that."

"No you can't. No no no no no no no no no no no no no no no no no no no no no no no no no no no no no no no —"

"Stop that."

"— no no no no no no no no no no no no no no NOOOOOOOOOOOOOOOOOOOOO."

"Are you done?"

"You smell like COW POO."

"If I was your mommy, I'd turn you right over my knee and spank you."

"No one's my mommy."

"That's not true. Now stop your silliness and listen to me. Children's Aid is trying to find your natural parents, your real mommy and daddy who have an obligation to support you. We found your father, Dorie. Mr. Luke T. Price, in Toronto."

"He's dead."

The lady is quiet a moment. "Who told you that?"

"Dunno. No one."

"You made it up. Well, that's called lying and it has to stop. You know what I think, Dorie? I think you are a good girl, a smart girl, who pretends to be wild and bad so you can get what you want."

"You can go now. I wanna watch TV."

"Why don't you tell me the real story about Kyle. The truth."

Dorie is quiet.

"That Kyle nonsense in the barn is the result of this household. That's just a fact. The shameless display of you, a young girl, to naive, susceptible boys who —"

"GO AWAY."

"I could take you with me. I could take you right now."

"FATTY, WHY'RE YOU SO FAT, DID YOU EAT A HORSE?"

Dorie looks right at the lady's face and the lady looks back with her mouth all twisted. She gets off the sofa and goes outside.

Then she comes right back in again and says, "Are they out there, in the field?"

"NO."

"They are. Something's burning."

The flames roar up and the heat sears Cam's face. They back off and watch the branches blaze in a swirling inferno till they collapse to embers around Luke's bulging body. His flesh bubbles and spits, like he's roasting more than proper burning. It looks to Cam like his body is swelled even more. Then, out the corner of his eye, he sees a car coming down along the windbreak.

"Wes. It's Gurneys."

They watch the big Merc come down slow and steady, bumping to a stop. There's just one Gurney inside: Beulah. She gets out and she's already jawing at them as she wobbles over.

"I found that child alone in the house in her underclothing. Disgraceful. You need to know that we found her natural father in Toronto. We will be in touch with him and if a meeting is suitable, the girl will meet him."

Wes gets a weird smile on his face. "If a meeting is suitable? I don't think that is suitable. What do you think, Cam?"

Cam can't even speak.

"I'm legal guardian," says Wes. "You're trespassing. Off you go now. Vamoose."

"You think this is a joke?" Then she's staring at the fire. "What in the name of —"

There's an explosion. Burning stuff hits Cam's face. He touches his cheek and black grease comes off on his fingers. Miss Gurney is flat out on her back. A gob of steaming stuff is in her hair. Wes goes and stands over her.

"Never seen a cow explode? Come on now. Time you went home." Wes starts tugging on her arm. "Let's get a move on. Get friggin' up, you goddamn … GET UP." Before she can get up, Wes is hauling her across the ground to her car. She's screaming but like she's so surprised she can't even get the breath out. Wes drops her beside the Merc. "Get in. Get in the car. You need help? You need friggin' help, you old bat?" He starts dragging her up.

"Wes, leave her. Jesus. LEAVE HER."

Wes stops and stares. He's not staring at Cam or anything, just frozen-like. Then he looks right at Cam and his eyes are like nothing Cam's seen before. Like Wes has gone missing. He moves away.

Cam crouches on the ground beside Gurney. She's crying now and saying "Oh Lord oh Lord" over and over.

"Miss Gurney? Listen. We're sorry about the cow. You never should've come down here. Stop crying, okay? Will you stop?"

Gurney wails, "That is a human being. You are burning a human being."

Wes and Cam look at each other, straight in each other's eyes. It's like the world stops. Except for Gurney bawling.

Cam says, "Why'd anyone burn a human? That's just crazy. It's a cow, Miss Gurney, swear to God."

Gurney hauls herself up to her knees. She grabs the car's door handle and gets up on her feet and finally in the driver's seat. Her hand goes for the starter, but Cam reaches in the window and knocks her arm away and pulls the keys out of the ignition.

Gurney goes quiet. She sits there staring with her baggy face all wet from crying, then she bends over the steering wheel and starts muttering prayers, begging Lord Jesus to spare her.

"Whatta we do, Wes?"

"Frig if I know."

"Thing is, no matter what, it's bad. We're in it real bad now."

"Yup. Goddamn straight to hell."

Gurney opens the car door. She gets out and she starts staggering back up along the windbreak. They watch her. She stumbles and falls, gets herself up and keeps going.

"She can't do that," says Wes. "Can't leave. Not a chance. Gimme the keys."

Cam hands over the car keys.

Wes gets in the Merc. "You coming?"

They drive up alongside Gurney and Wes talks to her while she trudges up the slope.

"Where you going? Because you're not going there. You're staying right here. Get you sorted out."

Gurney says nothing at all, not even a prayer. Just keeps wobbling along. Wes pulls ahead a bit and cuts left to block her path. She shrieks and falls down. Wes stops a little ways up the hill and they both turn and look out the rear window at her lying there. Cam can see her white legs.

Wes puts the car in reverse. He guns the engine and backs straight over Miss Gurney. Cam is screaming at him. Wes pulls forward, then slams it into reverse and runs right on top of her again. Cam jumps out of the car. He heads up the hill and keeps going until he's on the porch. His heart is pounding like it'll burst. He can still hear the sound of the revving engine. Dorie is on the loveseat, singing some dumb song and making her headless Barbie dance. Finally the engine sounds stop.

Cam goes into the house. He goes up the stairs to the bathroom and looks at himself in the mirror. At the black oily smudges on his face and shirt. His whole body is shuddering. He stares at his own face and it's like someone else is there, like he's separate from his own self. He yanks off his shirt and jeans and gets the taps going and he soaps up his face and hair and arms. He starts thinking hard. They're in it all the way now.

He comes out to the porch with fresh clothes on. Dorie's out on the grass, lying on her back and doing nothing at all except for her eyeball exercises. Blinky blinky blink. Stare. Blinky blinky blink. Stare. Blinky blinky blinky blinky blinky blinky ...

Cam sits on the loveseat. He's seeing blue sky and fluffy clouds and the giant old elm tree out there too, just like always, like the world never changes. But it's changed. Wes is a for-real murderer. Cam would be an accessory maybe. But Wes did it. The lady didn't even scream. Probably dead as soon as Wes hit her. So what happens now is she will be a missing person. Children's Aid will say she was paying visits to the Bliss place. And the OPP will turn up, asking them questions.

Now Wes's Ford is coming up from the marsh. Wes stops and shouts to Cam that he's heading out for more gas. So that'll make two humans, burnt up like cordwood — or three, counting Gramp.

scotch lake

THEY PACK CLOTHES AND FOOD in Wes's car and leave just as it's getting dark. Wes drives ahead in the Merc and Cam follows in the Ford with Dorie. Dorie is real quiet. Cam actually lies to her, says they'll be away only a few days, maybe a week. They're driving to Scotch Lake, a place Wes went with his mum and dad when he was a kid. Cam only knows it's somewhere far north.

Wes leads them along the back roads past Collingwood, then heads straight north on the highway through Parry Sound. They stick to the speed limit. Cam doesn't have a licence and anyways Wes's driving a stolen car.

Not too far from Sudbury, Wes pulls off on a road winding through rock hills. Cam follows the Merc onto a gravel turn-around by a dump. The headlights flash across old fridges and wringer washers and heaps of garbage. Cam's wondering what's up. Wes pulls to a stop and the car lights go out, then he's out of the Merc and stretching his limbs. Cam shuts down the Ford and gets out.

"Why're we stopped, Wes?"

"Merc's low on gas. Won't be a station open a few hours yet."

Wes takes a long piss in the weeds and Cam does the same, then he checks on Dorie. She's just waking up in the back seat.

"You need to pee, Dor? You gotta do it here."

Seems like Wes isn't in a talking mood. Cam wants to know what the plan is. Like, when will they go back to the farm? Ever? Did Wes do the burning right so there's nothing left? He was down there a long time but all he said when he came back, with blood all over him, was he took care of things and they had to leave.

"Wes."

"Yup?"

"I was thinking about the bones."

"Burnt 'em. That second batch of gas did it. Nothing but ashes now. Burnt Gramp's trailer, too."

"What about Gurney?"

"Didn't burn Gurney."

"What then? Buried her?"

"Now why would I do that? She's coming up the lake with us. Near gave myself a hernia getting her in the trunk. Thanks for the help."

"You're the one ran her over."

"You got it. I'm the one."

Wes goes silent again. The night is cool and the air completely still. Just crickets chirping and a few car sounds from over on the highway. The dump smell hangs around them. Dorie's back inside the car but she's quiet, too. Cam can see her face looking out the back seat window, just a white blob in the dark. Cam takes a look round the sky. No moon tonight, not a cloud anywhere. Only the stars. Even brighter than at the farm.

"Wes, what about money? If we run out of food, I mean, at the lake."

"I got money."

"How'd you —"

"Friggin' bank, where else. Couple days ago."

"How much?"

"Enough."

"But how we gonna —"

"Shut it, okay?"

Cam shuts it. After a bit he says, "You hungry? I could slice some of that apple cake."

"Naw. Dorie, maybe."

But Dorie doesn't want cake, either. Cam is feeling chilled so he gets back in the car. A little later Wes climbs back into the Merc. Cam's filled up with worry but he's so tired he eventually dozes off. When he wakes up, Wes is out having a whiz. The sky is getting light. Cam gets out and stretches. He opens up the trunk and takes out some juice and apple cake.

"Want some breakfast, Dor?"

There's no knife to cut the cake. They use a hunting knife out of Wes's tool kit. They punch holes in a tin of grape juice and drink straight out of the can, watching two raccoons nose around in the garbage heap.

Once they're past Sudbury and headed west, the day turns warm. Cam keeps close to the Merc and gets nervous when a car passes and gets in between. But Wes is good at slowing down so the in-between car passes him quick and Cam is looking at the Gurneymobile again. The plate says 47778-X. Cam figures that number will stick in his memory forever. Looks like lucky sevens didn't do much for the Gurney sisters.

Wes has worked out how much gas they need in the Merc to get to Scotch Lake and not any farther. He didn't say what the plan is, and Cam has stopped asking. Every question seems to make Wes irritated. They're both jumpy and there's no way not to be.

But when they stop to get the gas, Wes is all friendly and chatty. He tells the pump jockey a whole string of lies, like they're from North Bay and on a couple weeks' holiday, plan to do some fishing off Manitoulin. Cam's glad that Dorie's asleep, or she might've blurted out something dumb. Well, not dumb, but trouble.

Now they're stopped at a diner in Espanola. Wes is inside getting sandwiches so they can stop later by the road and eat without other folks staring at them, which is what folks always do, mainly because Dorie is so weird. But Cam knows they seem strange to regular people, anyways. Something about the Bliss family.

"How you doing, Dor? Hungry?"

"I hafta poo."

"Crikey. Why didn't you go at the gas station? Can you wait?"

"Mayyy-beee."

"When we stop to eat, then — not here."

Wes comes back and they head out on the highway. Pretty soon they turn north on a road that goes through a patch of farmland and then into woods and hills. A loaded logging truck goes by them, headed south. After a while, Dorie says, "WE GOTTA STOP." Cam taps the horn to alert Wes and pulls over.

While Dorie does her business, he and Wes stand looking at the trees and a creek that runs alongside the road. The water's crystal clear, rushing over rocks. The air smells like warm pine needles. But the thing is, it'll get cold soon, and frost and then snow, and how are they gonna survive in a cabin in the woods?

"Wes …"

"Least she didn't crap herself."

"Whatcha mean? She never does that."

They watch the creek. Cam sees a sandy spot not too far away by the water. There's even a log they could sit on.

"Wes, why don't we eat now? I'm starved. There's a nice spot there."

"Makes no difference."

"Course it makes a difference."

"We got a dead old lady in the trunk and you wanna have a picnic."

"Well, why not? Go get the sandwiches, okay?"

They eat their thin ham sandwiches with mustard squeezing out, not like at home where Cam slices it thick off a real ham from Elora Butchers. Wes's mood gets better. He starts talking about Scotch Lake.

"There's Whiskey Lake, too. We'll be driving right by it. Dad took me fishing there. Used to joke how if you fell in and drowned, you'd die happy."

"Guess you would in Scotch Lake, too."

"Yup, never tried it, though. Dad drank beer. And there's no Beer Lake I know of."

They eat and stare at the rushing creek water. There's a couple chipmunks chattering at them from a tree. Wes is saying how the lakes are full of trout and muskies and pike and they'll be living on fried fish and mushrooms fresh from the woods and even blueberries.

"Now that you got the knack for pie-making."

"Sure, Wes, and where'll we get flour and sugar?"

"IGA. Down in Willard. Went right by it on the highway."

"Why didn't we stop?"

"Jesus, Cam, use your noggin. We go back after we ditch the Merc, plus we check first what we got in the cabin. Pretty sure there's flour and sugar — canned goods, too. I'll drive down to-morrow morning."

They stick to the paved road awhile, then Wes makes a left and they're bumping along on a winding track. Sometimes they have to go at a dead crawl and steer around bumps of bedrock sticking up. They meet a pickup coming out and have to pull hard over into the brush while he squeezes by. The man waves at Cam as he goes past.

Eventually Wes turns off to the right. The way is not so rough here, winding through tall pine trees and a brown carpet of needles. Eventually they crest a hump, and down below is a lake with a wooden dock and two trucks parked. Probably gone fishing. Wes keeps following the track around the lake, then they veer away and they're going through thick woods again.

"Are we almost there?"

"I think we're close, Dor. That must've been Whiskey Lake."

The trail gets narrower. They pass a rusted-out old jalopy with the doors hanging off. Then they're there. The cabin is a real log one. The roof has moss all over it. The windows are shuttered up. Wes stops on a flat patch of rock and Cam pulls in beside him. They all get out and Dorie starts exploring right away, running down past the cabin to the lake. Cam follows her. There's a little pebble beach and a sagging dock. Scotch Lake is closed in by hills and craggy rocks. The cabin's at the end of a narrow inlet.

"You stay off that dock, Dor!"

"Naw," says Wes, "only two foot deep there. She's fine."

Wes tramps off into the trees. He comes back and undoes a padlock bolting the door. He turns to Cam. "Let's take a look."

Wes disappears inside. When Cam comes in, he's already unlatching the windows and shutters and letting the light and air in. The cabin has a wood and mouse smell. First thing Cam notices is a stuffed fox with snarling teeth. He can see right away it's a bad stuffing job. Maybe it was roadkill or something. One eye is way too low and the legs are bent funny. Wes is checking the beds.

"All looks good and dry," says Wes. "Okay, first thing, I show you where the key's hid," and he leads Cam through the trees to a hollow stump. "The crapper's out the other way."

When they come back, Dorie is inside, patting the fox and talking to it.

"Is it real, Wes?"

"Sure it is, Dor. My grandpa made it. Used to be foxes around here."

There's two narrow beds and a double bunk against the walls. There's open shelves with canned goods and storage tins. There's a washstand with a drainboard and a tin wash basin, and a little brass tap attached to a pipe coming out of the wall. Cam turns on the tap and nothing happens.

"Gotta fill the cistern, Cam. Then we got running water to last."

"Whatta we cook on?"

"Use the grill pit when the weather's good. For inside we got a little Coleman stove, and the wood stove here, too." Wes pats the iron stove by the door.

Cam sees there's a full bin of split wood beside it. Seems Wes's family took care of the place. The floor even looks swept. There's a varnished pine eating table in the middle of the room with an old kerosene lamp on it and salt and pepper shakers. Light from the lake-side window reflects off the honey-coloured wood.

Cam's trying to think how he'll make meals and do the washing up and so on. It could work out all right, except there's no electricity and no fridge.

"Grab that bucket, Cam. We'll get the pump primed. Then we're going fishing."

"What about the Merc? We just gonna leave it there?"

"Why not. She'll keep one more night. I got it worked out, don't you worry."

There's a metal tank bolted up on the back side of the cabin with some steps going up and a hand pump rigged. That's the cistern. Water for drinking and washing comes right out of the lake. Wes goes down to clear debris from the end of the pipe. Once they get it going, the water gushes out with every stroke. When it's running clear, Wes unscrews the cap on the tank and they take turns pumping till it's full.

"This tankful will last a few weeks if we don't waste it."

"We gonna be here that long?"

"Sure we are. Longer. Got everything we need."

Wes goes round the corner of the cabin. He reaches up under the floor and finds a key, and he goes and unlocks a rowboat chained to a tree by the dock.

"Got a little outboard inside, but we'll use the oars for now. Ever row a boat, Cam?"

"Course I did. At church camp."

They're out on the lake, far enough that Cam can see it going off in three or four directions. The shore looks steep and rocky in most places. The water's glassy smooth. Cam's rowing slow and gentle and Wes has a couple lines cast off. Cam is facing back toward the cabin where the sun is shining low into the birches and pine trunks and lighting the mossy roof bright green. He can see Dorie on the shore by the dock. They told her she can go in up to her knees and not any farther and she's not allowed to mess around with anything. They'll be out there watching her, and she has to stay in their sight. No chance she's allowed in the boat with no life jacket.

Only time Cam went fishing was at Simcoe church camp. He didn't get the hang of it too well, but he liked the fried fish after. Wes says they'll catch a decent dinner in no time. He's right. He reels in a rainbow trout, then a good-size smallmouth bass. He knows all the names. He snags another bass and they're set for a dinner feast cooked on the grill. Cam's already thinking of the cans of creamed corn he saw on the cabin shelf.

Wes gets a wood fire going in the BBQ pit. He scales and cleans the fish. Cam and Dorie watch him scoop the guts out with his fingers and toss them in the fire, where they bubble and sizzle.

"Don't want skunks and porcupines coming round for that. Bears, even. Best to burn it."

When the fire's down to hot coals, they put on a pot with the creamed corn. Wes gets out a special griller that squeezes the fish between wire mesh.

Cam is seeing a new side of Wes: he's really happy to be here and show them the cabin life and how he knows all the ins and outs. It feels like a holiday, as long as they don't think about dead Beulah Gurney and the fact they can't go home.

21

WES STARES INTO BLACK WATER. The drop from the edge is straight down, maybe thirty feet to the surface, and God knows how much deeper to the lake bed below. When he was a kid, teenage boys used to dive here. They got hurt sometimes if they hit the water wrong, but never from hitting the bottom. The boys said there was an old car down there, old from the time when Scotch Lake Hunting Lodge still dumped its bottles and cans and other junk, any trash that would sink, right here off the cliff.

He goes and sits in the Ford to think things through. There's not a lot to think about, really. They'll come late at night, drive the last part with the headlights out and rig Gurney's car to drive itself off the edge. He'll chain or bolt the trunk lid shut just in case, take the plates off and sink them somewhere else. From where the Ford sits right now, the path to the cliff is basically bare rock, not too rough and even sloped slightly toward the water. It'll do for the Merc's final run.

The lake's deserted. They did see one other boat out fishing last night, too far away to bother waving hello. Labour Day weekend is past and folks have gone home. The whole of Scotch has only five or six cottages, mainly out the west side where the road comes in from Elliot Lake way. No one keeps up the old lodge road to the east anymore.

He sits staring out at the lake, at the point of land marking the entry to their cabin inlet. Right now from this spot, the lake looks untouched, like no humans ever got to it. But there's all that junk on the bottom, and more going right back to Indian times. Centuries of human debris. Probably more than one rusted old banger got driven off the cliffs around here.

They shouldn't have stopped on the highway. Not for gas and not at the diner. He could've parked the Merc on a back road with Cam and gone in his own car for food and a couple cans of gas. He needs to plan better. Still, no point losing sleep. How did they get in this godawful mess? A month ago everything seemed hunky-dory. It's the curse of the Blisses.

First thing tomorrow, he has to phone Doug Johnstone and feed him a cock-and-bull story. Plus he never did get back to him about settling the new land lease. They'll soon be needing those cheques.

✣

Wes parks the Ford behind a big truck at the back of the IGA lot. He does the grocery shopping then walks next door to Willard Legion Hall with a pocket full of change. There used to be a pay phone in the downstairs bar. Hasn't been near the place in ten or twelve years, but he doubts it's changed much. His dad sometimes drank there in the summers, before the emphysema got him.

Sure enough, the phone is still there, and the same old corkboard riddled with thumbtacks. Doug's number pops into Wes's mind as soon as he pictures it on the wall at home. He dials zero and feeds coins into the slots until the operator says it's a go, then listens to endless rings and finally hangs up. His change clatters back.

An older guy is shuffling glasses behind the bar. Looks like Wes is the only customer.

"You serving yet?"

"Close. One o'clock, give or take. You a member?"

"My dad used to come in here, till he passed on. We had a place up Whiskey Lake way."

"What'll you have? Fifty, Export, IPA?"

"IPA, thanks."

Wes drinks his beer and then tries Doug again. He gets Roy.

"Roy, it's Wes Cody. I'm ready to discuss the new lease arrangement."

"What'd that be?"

"Well, it's not settled. Doug talked some figures …"

"Gotta talk to Doug."

"Okay, you do that and I'll —"

"It's you gotta talk to him."

"Is he there?"

"Try later."

"Any idea when he'll —"

Roy's already hung up. Wes suddenly wants to rip the phone off the wall. Instead he just swears. The barman looks him over as he walks out.

He heads along the street to the post office to arrange a mail-box. Soon as he's inside, he can see the clerk is the same chirpy old fella he remembers, gabbing away at some woman. As Wes is waiting for him to finish, he spooks. He turns around and heads straight out the door.

Back at the legion, he has another beer to ease his nerves. He's thinking how close he came to a major screw-up. No way can he have a postbox here. He'll have to get it down the highway some-place, Iron Bridge or Thessalon; give them a false name, too.

A few guys are shooting the breeze now in the barroom. The TV has a CFL game on. Nursing his IPA, Wes puts his mind to what he'll tell Doug about why they're away. Obviously more than just a little holiday — long enough that they'll be wanting the lease cheques posted north. Whatever story he tells Doug will get out to Kate McKieran, too, and half the county, likely.

He didn't kill Luke Price. Never wanted to, either. But the Gurney woman ... The whole situation's giving him a pain in the neck, a real actual pain shooting up through the back of his head like he used to get when Gramp was beating on Cam. He cracks his neck back and forth a few times, but it's not much of a help, just makes the usual popping sounds.

The barman is watching him. "That's quite a trick."

Last night he hardly slept after the first hour or so. Woke up like someone shook him, like the rickety bed was bucking, just the way the car did when he drove over her body again and again, because he had to be sure she was dead, because the idea of her still alive when he got out and saw ... Well, he just had to finish it. Then he drove a few yards up the hill and sat a bit till he calmed down. He finally got out and went back to her there. Her skull was smashed. He had some picking up to do to get all of her in the trunk. Then a stop by the pump shed to hose off the wheels and undercarriage.

So last night, all of that came back to bounce around in his head. He finally went out and sat on the end of the dock, and later Cam called down was he okay, so he lied, "Yup, just dandy, Cam, you go back to sleep."

The barman's looking at him.

"Up Whiskey Lake, are you?"

"Yah, round about there."

"How's the fishing?"

"Good. Trout, bass, had a real feast last night."

"You'll land some muskies too, you keep at it. These boys here know where to find 'em. How big was that muskie, Ern?"

"Twenty-seven pounds. She was a beaut."

"Couple these boys might remember your dad. What's the name again?"

"Fred. Fred Paisley."

The old guys look at Wes with blank faces.

A bit later, he tries Doug and gets Roy again. He says Doug'll be back in ten minutes or so. Wes phones in fifteen and thank Christ, Doug picks it up. They settle the lease amount and Doug says he'll drop the first cheque.

"You gotta send it, Doug. We're here at my mother's place."

"Where's that?"

"Up north. She's taken sick."

"Thought your folks were Hamilton way."

"She moved. I'll let you know the P.O. box. You can send October, too."

"Guess you heard about the McKieran boy."

"Heard what?"

"Gangrene in his hand. Had to take two fingers off. Kate said a crapload of stuff about your girl, too, like she was responsible."

"The woman's a barefaced liar. That boy molested Dorie in their barn. What he did to our girl, I can't even ... It'd make you puke, Doug."

"Try me."

"Well, you figure it out."

"You gonna report him?"

"He'll talk a load of lying crap just like his mommy."

"What'd he do to her?"

"Can't tell you."

"What the hell?"

"Doug, I'm feeding a pay phone here, I gotta go. I'll call you."

Wes hangs up. The whole bar is staring at him, then they act like they're not. He orders another beer. He's starting to wonder if he's fibbing too much, digging himself in. Why does he have to say anything except they'll be away awhile? Nobody's business, anyway.

When he gets back to the cabin, it's near sunset and Cam's mad at him for taking so long.

"Jeez, Wes, I can smell the beer on you. I was worried. We'd be stuck here."

"Stuck how? Here I am. I took care of stuff. I phoned Doug Johnstone, went to IGA, I even got Cheezies for Dorie. You left that off the list."

"Jiffy too?" says Dorie.

"Jiffy too."

Cam asks about the lease money.

"Doug's sending the lease cheques up here. We're set."

"Set for what?"

"Couple months."

"November? We'll be snowed in by then."

"Christ, you're a real worrywart. Better get supper going — we gotta sink the Merc tonight."

❊

They get Gurney's car sunk and first thing in the morning head back to the cliff to have a look in the daylight.

Cam makes Dorie stay in the Ford and he goes with Wes to the edge. The morning's cool and breezy. They stare down at the water. They can see it down there through the waves, a big, squarish light-coloured thing so far down you almost think you're imagining it. Almost.

"Well, shit," says Wes. "Friggin' crapola. You see that?"

"Yeah, I do."

"If the lake's calm, you know, like glassy calm, that's gonna look like a car down there."

"Wouldn't ever get glassy calm here, Wes. It's all open water, not like our little inlet."

"Hope you're right."

"Real windy here, waves bouncing off the rocks. It's choppy."

"Yah, I guess."

"They'll never find her. You picked the perfect spot. Let's go."

Cam is spooked, thinking about Gurney's corpse down there. He gets in the car and waits for Wes to stop pacing and staring over the edge.

He knows Dorie figured things out. Of course she did. The Merc was starting to stink. Then Wes made her stay away while he punched holes in the metal and put some bolts in to make the trunk secure. They sat her down this morning and gave her a serious talking-to about keeping it all secret. They told her it was an accident, just like Luke Price. Cam doesn't like lying to her, but the truth is too much.

"Wes, let's go!"

Wes comes back and sits behind the wheel, staring out. His jaw muscle is twitching like mad. He looks at Cam.

"Kids go diving here. They been doing that since forever. They'll be going down there to poke around."

"Wes, nothing we can do now, put it out of your mind. You'll just make us crazy, right? So stop."

Wes presses his forehead on the steering wheel, like he wants to push the bad thoughts out.

"How'd I get us into this? Jesus, how stupid. GODDAMN STUPID."

"Wes, it's okay. Nothing we can change."

Cam looks at Dorie. She's got her eyes squeezed shut. Then she bursts out: "I'm glad she's DEAD."

"Don't say anything, Dor. Not to anyone, not ever. Promise?"

"Never ever. I promise."

They sit quiet, except for Wes kind of moaning to himself.

"Can we go home?"

"We can't, Dor, not yet."

"I mean cabin home."

"Yep, we can do that for sure."

Wes starts the car, but his face looks awful. He's looking into the hell pit again.

22

DUST AND COLD GATHER IN the house. It has never been shut up like this. Never been without Blisses in it, not for a hundred years.

Here come Tom and Kyle through the corn stubble. They'll find the rabbit trap or not, but get a good look at the place while they're at it. Kyle is healing from his wounds. His left pinky and half his ring finger are gone — not so strange for a farm boy. He's back to school now and showing off his scars.

They go up to the house and peer in the porch windows.

"They left Sugar Pops on the table, Kyle."

"Want some?"

Kyle pulls open the screen and turns the doorknob. The door opens a wee crack. Bolted from inside. They go round back and find the cold room door padlocked. Then they pry a window and they're in. Their boots leave field mud across the sitting room and kitchen lino. The cereal box is almost empty. No milk in the fridge, just jam jars and mustard and it's shut down anyhow and smells. They eat the Sugar Pops and some Saltines from the cupboard. Kyle goes upstairs while Tom stays and snacks on crackers.

Kyle is in Cam and Dorie's bedroom. He opens the dresser drawers. There's boys' underwear and little-girl panties. He stands looking at the rumpled beds and the flowery wallpaper. He lies down and, thinking of Dorie, he starts getting a woody, but then Tom is clomping up the stairs.

They go out to the barn but can't see the trap anywhere. It starts raining hard, so they sit in the hayloft awhile.

"I don't care about the trap, Tom. We got a bunch still. Nearly killed me, anyhow."

"More like her nearly killed you."

"That's it. She set it there hidden. And she's watching behind the tree, laughing at me."

"Queers."

"Dorie can't be queer, dummy."

"Sure she is. Not normal."

"Crikey, queers aren't girls. It's when guys suck another guy's wiener, don't you know that?"

"That's what Cam and Wes do?"

"Sure, I seen them in the woods."

The rain is pouring down buckets. After a while, Tom says, "Guess Cam and Wes are going to hell someday."

"They can go right now."

23

"WES, WE GOT TO GET in some more food. Maybe find a laundromat, too."

"I won't be doing laundry."

"Then gimme the keys and I'll go. I'll pick up a few beers too, if you like."

Wes hands Cam the keys. "Take it easy on the way out."

"I drive more careful than you."

"Yah, so prove it. And don't go talking to folks."

"You're the one went drinking beer at the legion hall."

"Don't start on me."

"You might do a little cleaning up here, if you're not that busy."

"I'll chop some firewood, how's that? Maybe catch us some supper, too."

Driving past the dock at Whiskey, Cam gets a friendly wave from two anglers loading a boat. Folks wave at them, but it's over three weeks here and so far they only had any actual chat with a grey-bearded guy named Gus who lives at the abandoned lodge. Wes knows him from back when he and his folks spent the summers here. Wes says Gus used to be a jailbird but he went straight.

The lodge owners let him stay there to watch the place and keep kids from trashing the buildings, but they do anyway.

Gus even spends winter on the lake. So Wes has been talking about how they can do that, too — load up with canned goods and firewood and rough it like the pioneers, do some ice fishing, trap some rabbits. But that'll mean snowbound November to April, maybe longer. They're already getting frost in the mornings.

All Cam can think is there won't be any place to go except one room, and Dorie won't have TV to keep her quiet, and how will Cam get books? There's just three books in the cabin — two stupid *Hardy Boys* mysteries and a fly-fishing book more boring than not reading at all. He should've brought along Ray Bradbury and his other library books, even though it'd be stealing. Instead he's been reading soup cans and the Coleman stove instructions. There's a thing called cabin fever. People go loony. Especially if they partly are already.

Now he's driving the rough and stony stretch that leads to the main road south. Cam can see he's got a knack for this — he's not impatient like Wes. He even stops at the really bad spots to scan ahead and estimate the best way to steer around the humps and potholes and sharp stones. It's like a game of skill but a serious one. It helps make his mind clear and chases away the worry thoughts. When he gets to the paved road, he's almost disappointed.

At the stop sign he waits for two logging trucks to go by before he pulls out, then he wishes he'd had the gumption to scoot out ahead of them like Wes would've done.

But Cam's not a risk-taker like Wes, and Wes is why they're for-real criminals now and about to spend a whole winter in the frozen north woods. And it's why Cam is stuck now behind two trucks, choking on diesel fumes.

The IGA cashier tells him where the laundromat is. He coasts downhill from the highway along Willard's main street, looking at Lake Huron spread out there at the bottom with the sun glinting on it and a huge island that's gotta be Manitoulin.

Cam's never been in a laundromat before. They always used the wringer washer in the cellar and hung stuff out on the line. How will they wash clothes when they're snowed in? How will they wash at all, without a bathtub and hot water? The lake's already pretty cold for swimming. He watches someone else's laundry spinning around in a big electric dryer.

A lady shows him how to buy soap from a vending machine and put the quarters in the washers. Then he's got nothing to do but sit. The lady sits down on the bench beside him. She's a glamorous type. Got tight yellow pants on and red lipstick. He can smell her perfume — like cherry candy.

She has a magazine and while she flips through, looking at the pictures, she says to him, "You folks on holiday here?"

"Yep. Yep we are."

"Where you staying?"

"Got a cabin. I mean, my cousin does."

"Well, that's nice." She looks right at him and smiles. Her eyebrows look drawn on her face, arched up. "You're not back to school now?"

"They took me out. Had to help my gramp."

"I see. I'll bet you're a farm boy."

"Well, you're right. But we don't farm now. Land's rented out."

"Well well ..." says the lady.

She keeps staring at him. There's no one else in the laundromat. She's acting kind of weird, Cam thinks.

"My name is Cindy."

"Okay."

"And your name ..."

"Uh, Jimmy."

"I hope you don't mind my saying, Jimmy, but you must be the first young man I've ever seen doing laundry here. I mean young as you. You must be —"

"Seventeen."

"And how old do you think I am?" She kind of wiggles her head and blinks a few times.

"Jeez, I dunno."

"Not so much older than you."

Cam doesn't believe that. Cindy looks maybe thirty, or even older.

"I noticed you have a car. I could use a lift home, if that's all right. My car is kaput and, well, I'm not far, just along the highway."

Cam stares at her. "How'd you get here?"

"I drove. That's my little Falcon out there. Kaputski." She pouts.

"Uh, I think maybe ..."

"Do you happen to like banana cream pie?"

Cam doesn't know what to say.

"It's not much to offer but, seeing as you're driving me ..."

"I made a bunch of apple pies. Like my gran used to."

Cindy stares at him. "Well, aren't you talented."

❊

Cam lies in bed, listening to Wes snoring. The strange thing is he's never slept with Wes in the same room, or not more than once or twice — only with Dorie, and she never snores. Maybe he'll get used to it.

Wes made a comment about the perfume smell. Cam should've thought of that, maybe washed himself after. But he still told Wes the actual truth: a lady in the laundromat helped him and the whole place smelled from her perfume.

With Cindy, it was different from Wes. Cindy did the same things with his wiener, at first, but then it got completely not like Wes, not like a guy at all. She was softer. She had real lady breasts. Her skin was smooth. He didn't know what to do. Cindy did everything. She guided him.

She made him wash first. The shower curtain had flying birds on it, parrots maybe. She dried him with a pink towel. In the bed she sucked him and played with his nuts. That was like Wes except her nails were sharp. Cam felt like it wasn't real. Like he was a little kid watching from inside himself. Then Cindy put a Sheik on him. He never saw them before except in the box high up at the drugstore. But he knew what it was.

With Dorie around all the time, he and Wes haven't done anything since they got here, except just once out in the woods. Now he's wanting Wes. He wants him so bad all of a sudden. He reaches down beside the bed and feels for a sock. Then he does what he has to do, under the sheets. When he squirts he tries not to make a sound.

CAM'S WASHING UP THE LUNCH things, watching Wes and Gus out front. Wes is in Gus's old pickup, revving the engine hard while Gus has his head stuck under the hood. Gus is cursing like no cursing Cam's ever heard before. He can hear it right through the cabin window. Thick smoke is blasting out the tailpipe, blue smoke, and that means Gus needs a ring job or worse. Meantime Dorie's complaining she's bored and wants to go home.

"We're staying the winter here, Dor — how often I gotta tell you? Go play outside."

"It's cold out."

"Have a Fig Newton."

"THEY'RE GONE."

"Well, that's tough titties."

"You're a meanie."

Dorie puts on her jacket and goes out. Cam can hear her banging on the cabin wall. They stopped buying Cheezies because Dorie ate a big bag in one go and got sick, and now she ate a whole pack of cookies since yesterday. Cam would paddle her for real, but the paddle is back on the farm.

They play the transistor radio every day around suppertime to get the news, just in case. But there's still nothing about a missing Gurney or Luke Price. Wes says it's good news. Cam says it's only because there's other news more important. For instance, the girl kidnapped outside the Paisley 4-H whose body they just found in a suitcase in the Neustadt dump. But OPP could be looking for Gurney and Luke, they just don't know.

Gus bangs the hood shut. His hands are black with grease. Cam goes outside. Gus isn't swearing such a blue streak now. He's just gone back to his regular fuckin' this and fuckin' that.

"Shit on a brick, I'll just put new seals on the thing. Stop the fuckin' block leak, anyhow."

Wes says, "You might wanna open that block right up, take a look. Might get a blown piston otherwise, the way she's running."

"You a mechanic?"

"Just sayin', Gus."

Cam's gone over to look at the snowmobile in the back of Gus's pickup. The lodge owners got two Ski-Doos before they went bust, so Wes is making a deal with Gus to rent this one for the winter. He already paid Gus to fill the oil tank behind the cabin so they don't have to chop wood to heat the place. They still have to figure a system for water. The cistern hose is already freezing up some nights.

They have to be careful about going out. Can't let anyone see them together, and especially not with Dorie. Wes told Gus not to talk about them to anyone, said they're hiding out from some relations who want money. Today Wes gave Gus a bottle of Crown Royal for encouragement and that made Gus smile and show his rotten teeth. He has horrible breath. It's like something died in his mouth. Sometimes there's food stuck in his beard. Dorie won't even go near him.

DORIE'S LYING IN THE COLD cabin in the dark with the blankets pulled right up to her nose. The dark is slowly getting lighter because it's morning. She's looking at the roof beams above her bed and she's thinking of the farm. In her head she can see the rose wallpaper in her and Cam's room, and the Black Horse Ale horses stuck on the closet door, all going the same way. She misses them, but she can remember the horses and be right there with them in her mind. She can even smell the eggs and sausages cooking in the kitchen. Cam mixed the cut-up sausage in with the scrambled eggs and she ate it with toast and butter and jelly. She's tasting it right now.

Wes rolls over in his bed and the metal end of his bed bangs against Dorie's, and that brings her right back to the cabin and their stupid life here. Wes farts, a long one like a zipper. Then he throws the blankets off and sits up, rubbing his face.

"You awake, Dor?"

"Yip."

Wes is pulling his jeans on. "Jesus, it's a 'frigerator in here. You want oatmeal?"

"I want eggs."

"We're outta eggs."

"When are we going home?"

"You start that, I'll smack your backside, I'm not kidding."

Wes turns on the oil heater and goes outside. The heater makes a warm, slippery oily smell in the cold air. She likes if she can just stay in bed toasty warm with the covers up while Cam makes breakfast. But Cam's still hiding under his blankets, so today she's getting lumpy oatmeal with boring white sugar. Wes comes back inside, doing up his fly.

"We got an inch of snow out there."

They eat their porridge with Cam still sleeping. Then Wes says he's driving down to Willard to stock up in case they're snowed in — radio said it'll be storming tomorrow. So Dorie is left there with Cam snoring.

She gets up and has a pee in the pee pot, then she gets on her galoshes and parka and goes out to the snowy world. She dumps her pee where Wes left a yellow hole in the snow. They don't use the outhouse except for number two. If it's dark Cam takes her up the path with a flashlight in case there's animals. She hates the freezing-cold wood seat. Cam waits outside, shining the light for her through a crack.

She goes down to the water. The snowy dock has animal footprints on it but way too small for a bear. Dorie would like to see a bear but only from inside or in the car. She looks out across the lake. The sky is solid grey. There's no wind at all. No waves but the water is still moving. There's thin ice in the shallow parts around the beach stones. It's so quiet. There's a bird squawking far far away somewhere. She can hear Cam moving inside the cabin now. She picks up a stone and throws it. It hits the water, *plop*, and the rings spread.

Wes said the lake will freeze solid and he'll put a shed, a hut, on the ice with a hole for fishing. He said if you bring the Coleman lantern, the hut gets warm like indoors. The fish he catches are good. Wes knows how to cut them on the plate and lift all the bones away with the head so the fish eye isn't staring at them saying, *Don't eat me!* They have tartar sauce, too, from a jar. Cam made her a fish and tartar sauce sandwich for lunch. It's not like the farm here without TV and it's been raining a lot. But now it's snow and she can play outside.

Something's on the lake, way out. It's a boat. She hears the motor, like a bee buzzing. It's coming closer. Dorie stares at it a long time. It keeps coming until she can see a person wearing a red toque. It's a man with a long beard. It's dirty Gus! He drives the boat right up to their dock. There's a big, dead animal taking up the whole front of the boat. It's got brown fur and horns. Antlers. It's cut wide open so Dorie can see meat and ribs and an empty space, the empty inside where the guts were. Gus is grinning with his brown teeth. The boat motor is putt-putting and blowing smoke.

"Where's your daddy?"

"Don't got a daddy."

"Well, go get him anyhow."

Dorie turns around but there's Cam, already coming down the path.

Cam stares at the gutted deer. He catches a smell, like it's not too fresh. Gus is lighting up a smoke.

"Got this here for sale. Fifty bucks. Innerested?"

"Where'd you get it?"

"Fella I know."

"We're not interested."

"I'll cut 'er up for you. Got the deep freeze coming, she'll keep."

"Nope, thanks anyway."

"Where's Wes?"

"Out."

"Well, fuck it. I got other customers. Fuckin' come to you first."

"Sorry, Gus."

Gus is already zooming away. They watch until the boat's just a dot and there's only the motor buzz and the Λ shape in the water. Cam looks at their own boat tied up, with a layer of fresh snow all over it, like it's covered in vanilla frosting.

They go back up the path. Dorie goes wandering along the tire tracks left by Wes.

"Don't go past the old jalopy, Dor." That's their rule for wandering.

26

THE THESSALON POST OFFICE IS one small room with a wooden counter and a barred wicket and a wall full of open pigeonholes behind it.

The mail clerk squints at Wes. "Name?"

"Haney. Tom."

The clerk adjusts his glasses and writes it on a file card. "Address?"

"We're just temporary here."

"Home address?"

"Not at the moment."

"You got a phone number?"

"Not at the moment."

"Okay, then." The clerk looks up. "Ten-dollar deposit."

"That's a little steep."

"You can tell Ottawa."

Heading to his car, Wes suddenly feels starved. Anyhow, he doesn't feel like doing grocery shopping back in Willard — it can wait. He crosses the slushy main drag and goes into a diner. He settles in a booth near the windows. There's more snow here than at the lake, wet and heavy and melting fast. The diner is cozy and smells like fried eggs and bacon and coffee. The menu on the paper placemat says they serve breakfast till eleven. He's in just under the wire.

He needs this away time. He likes his fishing time out on the lake, too, just himself. Dorie's getting more on his nerves, for one thing. He stares out the window. Raindrops start to hit the glass. By the time his order comes, it's a steady downpour, but for a little while he feels warm and calm and almost happy, dipping his crisp bacon in the warm egg yolk, sipping diner coffee.

A pair of crewcutted teenagers come in, lanky and blue-jeaned, wearing windbreakers too light for the weather. They're soaked, water dripping off their faces. They sit in the booth opposite Wes and turn to stare at him for a bit, then they completely ignore him. They're obviously brothers, twins even. When the waitress comes she has a towel for them to dry off.

As soon as the boys open their mouths, Wes knows something's not right with them. The words have a *waw-waw* sound, like they can't get their tongues working. They seem more like kids than teens. Otherwise they look grown up enough to be finished high school. Wes keeps casting glances at them. Good-looking boys. Still got some summer tan. Their squared-off buzz cuts are so blond they're almost white. He knows what they'd look like with their shirts off, their hard stomachs and —

"Top up your coffee there?"

"Yup. Thanks."

"Weather."

"Sure is."

Wes makes himself stare out the window while he finishes up. The waitress brings Cokes and plates of french fries for the boys. He lets her keep filling his cup.

When the boys seem about finished, he takes his chit to the cash and pays. He goes out to the car. In the rear-view, he can see the diner. The boys eventually come out and start walking in the other direction. He could offer them a lift. Why not? Rain's still pelting down. Then they turn down a side street and disappear.

He's back at the legion hall to phone Doug Johnstone. He's got a trunk full of food from the IGA and still a little cash left from back home, but they'll be needing the lease money soon. He tries Doug's number but there's no answer. By the time he connects, he's on his third brew.

"I'm using a friend's postbox, Doug, in Thessalon. Name's Haney, Tom. Don't put my name on it, just confuse the old bugger in there."

Wes waits a dog's age for Doug to find a pencil and paper and write it all down.

"Who's this Haney fella? I thought you were with your mother."

"Yep, we are. I'll want it in cash, Doug, soon as you can. Don't have a bank account up here."

"Not sending cash, Wes. You'll be crying back to me if it don't come through."

"Doug, you owe us two months already — what you quibbling about?"

"It's you's quibbling. You never cashed a cheque in your life?"

"It's complicated."

"Sure sounds it. You better know, too — Kate McKieran is saying stuff about you boys."

"Like what?"

"Don't really know how to put it."

"This about Dorie?"

"Nope."

"Well, what's she saying?"

"That you're not normal. Yah. Pansies, like. Said Kyle saw you out back with Cam, in the woodlot."

"And you believed her? Doug, she's crazy, you know that. They oughta cart her away."

"Just saying what she told me. And another thing is OPP came by your place. She saw the cars."

"She's a friggin' liar."

"Okay, Wes."

"Don't 'okay' me. The woman's up to her nose in goddamn Jesus-loving horseshit."

"Okay, Wes. But I got to tell you, so you know. If OPP is there again, and I'm at your place there, and they're asking after you, I'm gonna have to tell them you're up in Thessalon."

"You do that, Doug. We got nothing to hide, nothing."

"Okay, then."

"Friggin' right it's okay."

Wes hangs up. Every man in the legion hall is watching him as he goes back to his beer. He finishes it off. He'd like to have another, but he has to keep a clear head. He decides he's got to phone Kate McKieran. But he won't do it with all these geezers eyeballing him.

He stops at a gas station with a booth out front. He's got just a bit of change, but it should be enough. While the operator's looking up the number, he tries to calm his thoughts. Then the phone is ringing and one of the boys picks it up.

"Is this Kyle?"

"Yep. You want my mom, she's out."

"It's Wes Cody here."

"Whatcha calling for?"

"I'm on long distance. My mother is taken ill and we're up north here with her, but I'm calling to tell you something, you listening?"

"Guess so."

"Then listen good, you little snot. Whatever shit you spread around about me and Cam is gonna come back to you. You did not see me and Cam in our woods doing anything because it never happened. You oughta be whipped, telling lies like that. Do you even know what a queer is?"

"Sure I do."

"A queer is a sad, sick pervert who hangs around city bars and picks up little boys. We are farm people. We are decent and regular Bruce County folks. You and your kind put a bad name on every damn one of us. I don't give a sweet fuck how churchgoing you are."

"You're from Hamilton, everybody knows that."

"What, you think Hamilton is Queer Town? Where'd you get that, goddamn Sunday school?"

"You'll be in hell someday — I know that, anyways."

"You know what hell is, Kyle? It's right there in your house. You people got no right to judge us or anyone. You can damn well put your own fucking house in order. I ever see you again you better stay out of my way. You tell your mom the truth. You know it and she knows it. You are the fucking pervert, Kyle, except you do it with little girls instead of boys, am I right?"

"Shut up, I know you burned your gramp, I know OPP is lookin' for you."

"You know zero. You know who OPP is looking for? The killer of that poor little girl they found tossed in the dump last week, the Paisley girl. Cops think he was hiding in our woods. Makes me sick thinking about it, almost as sick as the idea of you with our little Dorie. You got any information about that girl, Kyle? I could get the police to come have a talk with you, no problem at all. Anything you can tell them about guys who mess with little girls?"

"I don't know nothin' about that girl."

"You are a little sicko is what you are, Kyle. You and your sick family. I think maybe it was you killed that girl. Wouldn't surprise me. Maybe OPP think so too."

"Sir?" It's the operator's voice. "Sir, you have one minute."

"I'm done." Wes jams the receiver down.

He spends some time in the car with his mind racing. Then, after a while, he starts to think clear. No more out in the public view. No more pay phones with nosy operators. No more legion hall. One more trip to Thessalon for the lease money and that's it. Then they're going it alone in the bush till spring.

He should probably tell Cam about the OPP, but he won't say a word about the queer stuff. Nothing to do with him and Cam. Those boys in the diner got him fired up, sure. Young guys always did, even when he was that age himself. But that's not about Cam. Thinking on it right now, he feels like he'd give his life for Cam. He would honestly do that.

He sits awhile there in the Ford. Big snowflakes start to come down, melting on the windshield. Then, out of nowhere, he's crying like a kid, before he can stifle it. He's crying for the shit he's got them in, and how much he'd like to make it right, and how much he hates the whole goddamn world out there.

DOUG SITS ON HIS IDLING tractor eyeing the burnt-out Dodge pickup. Headlights look like they might be worth salvaging. His eyes shift over to Sam's burning spot, where days of rain have pretty much swilled the ashes into the ground and left only black cinders, rusty bedsprings and such, some bones. Wes must've burnt a pig carcass or something. He can see a chunk of jawbone too big for a raccoon or badger. What the hell would they be doing with a pig?

Doug climbs off the tractor and ambles over to the cinder pile. He reaches down and picks out the jawbone and brushes away the ash and grit. Got a good set of teeth on it. He stares. If they're pig's teeth, this pig has had a fair bit of dental work.

28

WES TOLD CAM THEY HAD to have a talk. They're sitting out in the Ford where Dorie can't hear them. He starts up the car once a week anyhow to keep the battery charged, so they're even getting some warmth with the heater going.

They had a two-day thaw second week of November. Wes knew it was likely his last chance to drive down to Thessalon for the lease money. Over three weeks since he told Doug to send it, but he got there and the clerk told him nothing had come in. Driving back to Willard, he thought he'd been lucky not to find a cop car waiting for him outside the P.O. Then he started checking his rear-view every two seconds. In town he spent the last of his cash on food and a half-tank of gas.

In the car now outside the cabin, he tells Cam all the money stuff he's been keeping quiet about: They've got about three bucks to their name and no more coming. Enough food to take them maybe to end of January if they stretch it. They can't even fish right now, ice is too thin. Somehow they have to get through till spring.

Cam just stares at him. "We got to make Doug pay."

"Jesus, are you even listening to me?"

"Maybe it's still in the mail?"

"It never got sent. And I won't ever be going back down to that post office."

Wes watches Cam's eyes moving like he's thinking through it all and it's sinking in. He's got a scruffy beard now, like Wes. They changed how they look. Wes took the plates off the Ford, too — not that anyone ever comes by this way except Gus.

Wes says, "We'll get money somehow. I got a few ideas."

They sit quiet.

Cam is real still, staring out at the lake. He says, "We're never going home."

"Yah, sure we will, someday."

Cam shakes his head, one little twist, then he goes completely still again.

Wes says, "I'll take care of us. It's what I got to do and I will do it."

Cam gets out of the car.

Wes shuts down the engine and follows him. He says, "Cam."

But Cam is walking past the cabin, toward the water.

Wes follows. "Cam."

Cam goes out on the dock, right to the end. He stands there.

"Cam?"

"Leave me be."

"Come inside."

"I said leave me be."

Wes is washing up, glancing over at Cam on his bed staring up at the top bunk. He didn't say a word at supper, left half his food. At six they turned on the transistor radio. The entire news program was about President Kennedy getting shot. That was the thing finally made Cam speak. He said, "That'd never happen

in Canada." And Wes said, "Nope. We just run down old ladies."
Cam stared at him like he was nuts.

When Dorie falls asleep, Wes goes and sits on the edge of
Cam's bed. Cam won't look at him.

"Bad luck's what it is, Cam. Started with Luke dying on us."

"We should've taken him to hospital."

"He was stone dead, you said so yourself."

"Maybe."

"It's what they call fate. We got a curse on us."

"You're friggin' right on that."

"Gonna let me lie down?"

Cam slides over to make room.

CAM'S OUT BY THE CAR. They're using it for a freezer, but it's been sunny and mild a few days and now their pork chops and ground beef are getting on the warm side. Cam's cooking up a big batch of meat and hoping they'll get a deep freeze again.

He hears a snowmobile. When he looks, it's coming full speed across the lake. He recognizes Gus's red toque. Gus zooms right past the dock and up alongside the cabin. The snow cover is so thin the machine screeches on the bedrock. He skids to a stop beside Cam.

"Jeez, Gus."

"Jeez to you."

"You could've gone right through that ice."

"What the fuck do you know?"

"Nothing, I guess."

"Where's your brother or your cousin or whatchacallim? Gotta show you boys something."

"So show me."

Gus pulls a newspaper out and shows Cam the front page, full up with Kennedy and Lee Harvey Oswald.

"Know all about it, Gus. We got a radio, remember?"

"Not that. This!" He jabs his finger at the bottom of the page.

Cam sees a small headline: "Human Bones in Bruce."

He stares at it and feels his stomach flip.

"So? Where'd you get this? You read newspapers?"

"Think I can't read?" Gus starts reciting out loud from the paper.

Cam grabs it and moves away.

> Ontario Provincial Police in Bruce County have dis-
> covered burnt skeletal remains in marshy land at an
> area farm.
>
> "It appears they are not animal bones of any
> type," said Sergeant Gordon Fernie, of Walkerton
> Detachment. "We have determined that they are
> human, possibly more than one individual," he
> said.
>
> The OPP seeks two males recently residing at the
> property. The public is asked to report any know-
> ledge of the whereabouts of Wesley Patrick Cody,
> 28, or Cameron Campbell Bliss, 17. They are also
> believed to have custody of a young girl, Sgt. Fernie
> added.

Gus is standing beside him again. "That's you and him and your girl."

"So what if it is?"

"Sooo, I'm sayin' what's up? Sounds kinda wild."

Gus grins. His breath smells for real like a dog crapped right in his mouth.

"Gotta get Wes."

Inside the cabin, Wes is swearing to himself trying to light the Coleman stove.

"Wes, holy frig, read this." Wes ignores him. "Wes!" He shoves the paper in front of Wes's face. "They found Luke and Gramp, their bones."

Wes grabs the paper and reads the story. He doesn't say a thing, just looks up at Cam with his eyes staring.

"You said you burned them, burnt to ashes you said."

"Where'd you get this?"

"Gus. He's out there."

They go out. Gus is standing with his arms folded, watching them.

Wes says, "Come on inside, Gus. I got a few shots of rye left."

"Why should I?"

"I'm offering you a drink, buddy."

"Now I'm your fuckin' buddy? Woooo ..."

"Come on now, Gus. We go way back."

"I was never your buddy. Never your old man's buddy. I did stuff for him. For pay."

"We always treated you fair. Always."

"Yah." Gus looks at the sky. "Yah. Maybe." He goes and lounges on his Ski-Doo and lights a smoke. "Here's the thing. I'm thinkin' what would you do, I mean if OPP was lookin' for me instead, for a thing like ..." Gus shows his brown teeth. "Like what you boys did with them human bones."

Cam says, "They're not human. It's dead cows or, dunno, badgers and stuff. Or, like, an Indian graveyard maybe. Makes no sense otherwise."

"Cam's right, Gus."

"What a fuckin' crock. I know you sunk that car, that nice-lookin' Merc. I know I'm s'posed to keep my mouth shut. Why should I? Gimme a reason why."

"Whatta you want, Gus? Can't pay you. We're flat broke."

"Fuck you are."

"Turn the place upside down if you want. I got about two dollars on me. That's gospel. Don't know how we'll get through the winter."

Gus watches them a long time, sucking on his cigarette the way he does, with his brown fingers pressed against his puckered-up lips.

"I'm gonna keep quiet. But you owe me. Big time."

"Sure, Gus."

"How much rye you got in there?"

"Couple inches."

"Go get it."

30

MID-JANUARY, WES IS OUT IN the hut with four lines dropped. He's got two decent trout and a couple of big walleyes chilling on the ice and a Thermos of hot tea and a bacon-fat sandwich. The Coleman lamp is burning just enough to keep him comfy.

He bites into his sandwich wondering how much longer he can put off the food problem. He's fishing every day he can and giving all they don't eat to Gus, who has a deal going with the local ice fishers and Indian bands, selling their fish and game to supermarkets and restaurants.

He finally told Gus last week he'd appreciate a few bucks for his labour, or else some canned goods or a little fresh game, not a lot, but something, because they'll be completely out of their food stash in a couple weeks and why should he sit out on the lake every day for nothing? Not worth it. He said to Gus, "I got Cam and Dorie to take care of, can't just live on fish and rice."

Gus said, "Fuck you can — I do."

Yesterday Gus gave him two bucks. Then they agreed on two bucks for every hundred pounds of catch, depending. Gus does the weighing. He's a first-class bastard.

Cam came out to the hut with Wes a few times but he's not much help. They end up mostly bickering. The fact is they're getting real sick of eating fish. What Wes wouldn't give for a grilled rib-eye steak and a baked potato. He almost drools thinking about it.

Gus took the rented Ski-Doo back and kept every penny of the advance money Wes gave him. The one thing Gus does give them is fuel for the Coleman lamp, but it's only because if Wes freezes to death out in the hut, Gus loses. He claims the *Willard Sentinel* and the other papers around say the police are still looking for them, but he won't show them the proof. They haven't seen a paper in over a month, but there's never been a single mention of them on the radio. Gus is shitting them for sure. He's just playing them, stretching it out a while so he can make easy money. Sooner or later he'll report them.

Sitting out there in the hut, Wes thinks how Gus could disappear from the picture. Like crash his Ski-Doo right through the ice and drown himself, or maybe go full speed into some barbed-wire fencing and slice himself into hamburger meat.

❧

Cam keeps hearing it from Wes: *Things gotta change around here.* But Wes isn't doing a thing about it. They've been fighting about stupid stuff like who chops wood or washes up after supper, but it's not about that at all. And with Dorie around and no place to be alone, they can't even make up proper after a spat.

Aside from fish and rice at suppertime, they're living mostly on oatmeal and griddle cakes. The last of their bread is mouldy. They've run out of coffee, peanut butter, sugar, and syrup. Lard and bacon fat are almost gone, too. Only cans they have left are two chicken gravy, one Heinz beans, and a tin of corned beef. Cam's saving the corned beef so he can do it with rice and gravy for Dorie's birthday coming up.

Wes is out on the lake all day most times. Goes out after breakfast and comes back late. Cam starts checking out the window when it gets dark. Then he sees the lantern swinging, way far out across the ice. Then it's lighting up Wes from the waist down, like it's just his legs coming, and the pail full of fish swinging in his other hand. The minute Cam sees the lantern winking, he puts the rice pot on. He makes sure there's hot tea ready, too.

He has an idea, maybe a crazy one. He can hitch a ride to town while Wes is out there. He can go to Cindy and tell her they're flat broke and ask her for a loan. Cindy said she'd like to see him again. She joked about it. "Sure hope you come back and do more laundry. I might need a ride home." What she knows about him is exactly nothing, except he's called "Jimmy." He never told her Wes's name or anything about Dorie. She would never think he was Cameron Campbell Bliss, running from the law.

He'll need to snowshoe out to the Whiskey Lake road and catch a ride from the ice fishers. He hears their Ski-Doos down there every day. Even if he can just get a lift to the highway, he'll be able to hitch down to town. He's got to plan it so it works all in one day. He'll leave Wes a note for sure, in case he gets back late, but that better not happen.

So Cam tells Dorie he'll be gone for the day and heads out one sunny morning as soon as Wes is out in the ice hut. The radio said no snow that day but it's pretty cold. He makes Dorie promise to stay inside. The coals from breakfast are still glowing in the stove and Cam puts the oil heater on low, too. Dorie knows how to shut it off if she gets too warm. He's wearing a heavy padded parka that looks like it's been in the cabin a hundred years.

Takes him an hour maybe to get to the road running alongside Whiskey, but a snowmobile comes by pretty soon: two Indians in deerskin coats and thick frost on their whiskers. They're happy to take Cam out to the paved road. They don't say hardly a word except is Cam looking to buy fish or venison. He says if he catches them on the way back, he might take the venison.

A big dump truck stops for him. He has to climb two steps just to reach the door handle. Turns out the driver is heading west out of Willard. He'll be going right past Cindy's place on the highway. The driver whistles and sings songs in French and talks about the weather but he doesn't ask anything that makes Cam have to lie.

Cam watches for the clapboard bungalow on the right, far back from the road with a few trees around it. He remembers it painted kind of minty green. When he's starting to think they went by it, he sees the bright green through the trees. The truck driver stops a little ways past the driveway and Cam walks back.

The mailbox by the road says *C. Murphy.* The driveway isn't plowed. He can see a car covered with snow. Looks like her little Falcon. He puts on his snowshoes and heads down the drive. The snow on Cindy's porch is untouched, drifted up against the screen door. He tugs it open and knocks not too loud a couple times. Then louder. No sound from inside.

He comes off the porch. Only marks all around are his own tracks. He goes to a window and peers in through the lacy curtains. Past the front room he can see the kitchen table where he had a slice of pie and milk. When he finished, Cindy asked if he wanted to take a shower, like it wasn't really a question. Cam stares a long time into the empty house.

He goes round the back. He knocks at the kitchen door, pretty loud this time. Maybe Cindy is sick. But no matter how much he knocks, nothing. What's he supposed to do now? He tries the doorknob. He looks around. He can see a house far away through some trees, maybe a quarter-mile or more. Nothing behind or on the other side, just fields and woods. He looks for a spare key. Digging in the snow near the door, he finds it inside a tin box of clothes pegs. He kicks his snowshoes off and lets himself in.

He closes the door so quiet behind him it's like he's afraid Cindy is sleeping. He stands there on the doormat by the kitchen. The house smells the way he remembers, sort of like apples. Perfume, too.

"Hello? Cindy? Helloo-oo ..."

He takes off his boots. He moves along the hall to the bedroom. The bed is perfectly made, not a wrinkle anywhere. The bedspread is pink with tiny blue beads all over it. The wallpaper is pink and yellow flowers. The curtains are lace like in the front room. There's a white and gold desk with a mirror — Cindy's vanity, with lipsticks and perfume and nail polish on it. The room has Cindy's candy smell. Cam stands there, remembering what happened.

He goes back to the kitchen. He finds crackers in the cupboard and he eats some with slices of hard butter from the fridge. Then he cleans up the crumbs and washes the knife and puts everything back where it belongs. He goes and sits in the front room where he can watch out the front window.

There could be money somewhere in the house. He's guessing it wouldn't be much. He'd be stealing. What's he doing here? He stares out at the blinding white snow and the sun glinting off cars on the highway. He could have a hot shower. That'd feel so good. Then he'll just go back to Wes and Dorie.

The bathroom door is closed. It feels stupid but he knocks.

"Cindy?"

He opens the door.

She's in the tub. The water is red. Her head and body are completely underwater, just her white knees sticking up. There's blood all over the side of the tub and the pink bathmat. A bottle is on the floor, a liquor bottle. He moves closer and stares. Cindy's hair is floating all around her head under the water. Her eyes and mouth are wide open.

He sees a razor blade on the floor near the bottle. He backs out and closes the door.

Cam sits watching the highway traffic. She didn't smell bad, not decayed at all. Maybe underwater, it hides the smell. But the blood looked fresh almost. Why did she do it? Maybe she had cancer or something. Cam wonders why he doesn't feel sad. Just kind of … interested.

He'd still be stealing even if Cindy is dead. But he thinks she would understand, because their situation is so bad. He starts looking for money. He checks under Cindy's mattress. He opens the top drawer of her dresser. Panties and bras. But there's no money in the dresser drawers or the vanity drawers, either.

On the vanity there's a framed photograph of two old people, Cindy's parents probably. Another one of a man in uniform next to the big propellers of a plane. Someone wrote at the bottom, *Cpl. Billy.* Beside the photos there's a little blue velvet box. Cam opens it. There's a plain gold ring and a silver one with *R.C.A.F.* and a flying eagle on it. He closes the box and leaves it.

In the front hall he finds Cindy's purse. Inside there's a red wallet with three one-dollar bills and some change. Well, that's it, then. He doesn't want to snoop anymore.

He should phone someone, to get her taken away. They can tell her family, too. He'll call from a booth in town. Not the police. A hospital maybe.

The sun's low in the sky by the time he gets back. He couldn't get a lift north from Willard for ages, then he had to snowshoe in almost to Whiskey before a skidooer happened by and took him right to the cabin.

When he comes in, he burns the note he left for Wes. He has a candy bar for Dorie he bought with Cindy's money, along with three bucks' worth of food he got at the IGA — exactly to match the food they've still got left, otherwise Wes will know he went out.

While Dorie's eating the candy, he makes her promise again not to say a word to Wes about him going away.

"Where'd you go?"

"Had to see someone."

"How come?"

"Doesn't matter. It didn't work out. C'mon, help me get water, okay?"

They go down to the lake. Cam breaks through the skim of fresh ice in the water hole and he fills two buckets. Dorie fills her two small plastic ones. Cam looks way across to the ice hut out the end of the inlet. Fish like it there around the submerged rocks by the point. It'll be dark in an hour or so and the lamplight will appear when Wes starts to trek back.

Cam wonders what Wes does with himself all day out there. He must be thinking. Cam knows that fishing is basically about doing nothing for hours and hours and that's why they like it — and why Cam never did. He wishes Wes would spend his thinking time figuring some way to turn things around so they have a proper life again.

31

IT'S FEBRUARY DEEP FREEZE AND Cam's cooking nothing but fish and rice. It'll be fish and nothing pretty soon. They gave up trying to trap rabbits. Only thing they caught was a porcupine. For Dorie's birthday they finished off the corned beef and chicken gravy, the last of their canned goods. Wes won't even talk about it. He's either out on the ice or sleeping in his bed. It seems to Cam like he's shut his mind off almost.

Wes said a while back that Gus started paying him a little bit for the fish. Said he's saving that, end of subject. He brings back his catch every night and Gus comes next morning and takes it all except for their dinner. One day Cam asked if they could use the other Ski-Doo sometimes, the one they rented, but Gus just laughed.

Cam's working up a new plan. He's keeping track of what Gus does and where he goes, catching on to his routine. Now and then he asks a question like he's just being a dumb kid. Between that and what Wes says, he's figured out that most every day, Gus is away from his place at the old lodge from early morning till toward mid-afternoon. He's out doing his rounds on Scotch Lake and Whiskey too, collecting from the fishers and trappers and delivering to distributors at a depot down the highway. Gus must be taking in pretty good money. Cam's pretty sure it would all come in cash.

There's nothing to stop Cam from snooping at the lodge, out the east side of Scotch. He and Wes took a look at the place from the boat back in October. He knows exactly where it is and he could get there by snowshoe easy as pie.

Gus comes for their fish in the first part of his run, usually not too long after sun-up. One morning after Gus has picked up their catch and Wes has gone to the hut, Cam fixes himself a Thermos of hot water and heads out and along the lodge road. Coming up to the turn-in for the place, he goes right past and cuts through the woods. He gets himself hid in the pines up top of the hill behind the lodge to keep a lookout.

He sits in the snow with his legs drawn up and his back against a tree, keeping his gloved hands in the parka's big side pockets. From here he sees the backs of the big lodge building and the cabins. Ski-Doo tracks go down to the lake. There's a tramped-down footpath in the snow between the lodge and a cabin close by to it. Wisps of smoke are coming out the stovepipe on the cabin roof.

The lake is dotted with huts and criss-crossed by snowmobile tracks. There's not much winter peace and quiet in the bush nowadays. Wes complains about it. He says when he was a kid, all you'd hear was the wind and birds, and sled dogs the Indians used. Some still use the dogs instead of Ski-Doos.

Cam is up high enough to see over to where Wes is right now, in his slope-roof shack made of old planks. He counts the huts that he can see all around the lake: seven. And there's others in the hidden inlets and over on Whiskey. Must be more guys than Gus collecting fish every day.

Cam tries to make his hot water last, but it's gone way too soon. It's windy so the sun doesn't help keep him warm. He and Wes rigged cardboard-and-masking-tape goggles with slits for the snow glare. He doesn't have to be squinting all the time to see clear, but nothing is moving around down at the lodge.

He starts to get sleepy. Has to shake his head or hum tunes from the radio so he doesn't drift off. He keeps remembering Cindy, the way she looked, and everything about her house. It comes into his head mixed up like a crazy dream. He gets up and walks around to clear his mind and find a new spot to sit.

He starts getting frost pains in his toes. Guessing from the sun, it must be mid-afternoon by now. No sign of Gus or anyone else. He figures he's froze himself long enough. If the weather is good tomorrow morning, he'll come back same time, keep a lookout for a little while and if it looks clear, he'll sneak into Gus's cabin. He gets scared thinking about it, but it's got to happen.

❊

Next morning, Dorie wants to know what's up. Cam's all ready to head out and she's looking at him with her head sideways like she thinks he's being bad and lying about it.

"Dor, here's the thing. We got no money. Wes is not doing a thing about it. I think I can get us some money, maybe enough to change things so we can get out of this place. It's a big maybe, not gonna lie about that."

"Where you going?"

"I'm going to Gus's place. I'm gonna take what he friggin' owes us. I'm sick of the way he's messing with us and it's gonna stop."

Cam goes out and bangs the door shut. He sits on the step, strapping his snowshoes on.

Dorie opens the door. "What if Gus gets mad at you?"

"He won't even be there. You stay inside and keep warm, okay? I'll be back soon, promise."

Up on the hill behind the lodge, he watches and waits. He knows for a fact that Gus is out the other side, probably on Whiskey

Lake by now. He came for Wes's catch at the regular time and then disappeared around the west point of their inlet, just like always.

So what is Cam waiting for? He's already decided that he'll take a look at the main building. Maybe Gus isn't the only one spending the winter down there. If there is anyone, he'll just pretend he's curious about the place.

He heads back through the woods to the road and comes into the lodge property on Gus's packed-down snowmobile path. He won't be leaving any snowshoe tracks if he can help it.

Then he's standing in the trampled path between what's got to be Gus's cabin and the big lodge building. He goes up the side steps to the long porch. The entrance doors are chained shut but it's stupid because the plate-glass windows right beside are broken. He could step right over the sill and get in. The sun is slanting in on log furniture and some big armchairs that look like animals got at them and tore them up.

Cam puts his head through the window and listens. Can't hear a sound.

"Hello!"

A rustling noise makes him jump. Out the corner of his eye, he sees a big bird fly out from under the porch roof.

He goes across to the cabin where he saw the chimney smoke. Traps are hanging by the door and bloody animal skins lie in the snow. Looks like Gus eats better than they do. The door is padlocked. Windows are shuttered up like the other cabins. Gus either lives in the dark or he locks up real tight every time he goes out.

Cam looks awhile for a key but no luck. He takes a good look at the padlock and hasp. Maybe he can jimmy it. He'll need a pry bar or something. He finds a claw hammer in a shed next to the lodge. Before he starts on the door, he takes a long look out at the lake and all around.

He gets the hammer claws wedged between the wood frame and the hasp. He pries and wrenches until the screws pop out of the old wood. He pushes the door open. The place stinks like cigarettes and Gus. He props the door wide for the light and waits for his eyes to adjust.

There's a table with opened food cans and a few empty whisky bottles. There's a workbench with a junked gas engine and other crap and tools all over. There's a bed with messed-up sheets and a filthy pillow, and another bed piled with boxes. There's even a fridge, an old-fashioned wooden icebox. But the door's wide open and the shelves are full of canned goods.

Where does he start? Gus's mattress? Cam stares at the grey sheets. He takes a look in the boxes on the other bed: dishes and pots, some girlie magazines. He looks under the bed: old shoes. He goes and lifts the blanket hanging off Gus's bed and peers underneath. There's a metal box. He gets down and drags it out. It's full of fishing tackle.

He spends a while searching through Gus's shelves and drawers and piles of old clothes. He yanks open a cupboard at the bottom of the icebox. There's some greasy-looking paper bags: *Bea's Chicken Shack*. He grabs one and opens it. Bingo!

He dumps the bag onto the table and counts the bills: $314. Cam's not even surprised. He knew Gus'd have a stash. There's six more bags. Cam gets them all out on the table. The second bag has more tens and twenties. He counts $545. He can't believe it. The next bag has $587.

He hears a snowmobile and his stomach flips. He goes to the door. It's out on the lake heading north — not Gus, either.

He doesn't do any more counting. He grabs a canvas duffle bag and puts the cash bags in it and tosses in a few cans of food and a box of pancake mix. For a moment he stands just staring out the door at the blinding white light.

Gus will blame them, of course he will. He'll cry robbery to the OPP, and on top of that everything that was in the papers about them, too. That'll be the end, the worst. They'll for sure go to jail and Dorie will go to Children's Aid. Cam gets crazy-feeling just thinking about it.

He doesn't have to look long to find a gallon can of kerosene. The place will go up like tinder. He stuffs firewood onto the smouldering embers of the stove. He leaves the stove door wide and stacks more wood on a chair shoved against the opening. He lifts off the iron cover of the firebox. Thick smoke from the fresh wood pours out. Before it catches, he pours kerosene over it and splashes more over the chair. As he jumps back, the stove explodes in flames. He pours more fuel over the floorboards and empties the last of it onto the beds. For good measure, he shoves Gus's eating table into the blaze.

He grabs the money bag and stands in the doorway watching the show. He feels the outside air rushing around him to feed the flames. The cabin is a storm of fire. Smoke and searing heat finally force him out the door. He straps on his snowshoes and heads up into the woods.

Wes comes out of the hut to take a leak and stretch his legs. He knows some guys just piss in the hole so they don't have to go out and freeze their dicks. To Wes that feels like desecrating his own dinner. On the other hand, 90 percent of what he catches goes straight to Gus and he'd be pleased to piss on Gus's dinner anytime.

Wes smirks as he lets loose into the snow in back of the hut. Coming round, he stares at the sky. Smoke is pluming up over the trees. He walks out to where he can see around the point to the lodge. Holy … That's Gus's cabin. Fire is blazing up through the roof and out the windows. Wes can't take his eyes off the flames.

Snowmobiles are heading toward the lodge. Are they actually worried about the old bugger? Nothing they could do, anyway, except watch the show. The one problem is there's almost no chance Gus is inside, getting burnt to a cinder.

32

CAM STANDS IN THE WOODS, watching the place burn. It's not long till the roof is collapsed and the battenboard walls are sagging into the inferno. Ice fishers are down on the shore now, watching the blaze. When a few come closer, Cam figures it's time to leave.

Heading back along the lodge road, he's tempted to stop and count the rest of the cash, but he knows he better keep moving. They've got to get away. If they could only just hop in the Ford right now and drive, keep on driving. But they can't. The car wouldn't get twenty feet. He stops, staring at the snowmobile tracks curving away through the bush. Then he turns around.

He's up in the woods again, watching the fire. There's three ice fishers still hanging around down by the dock. He can hear them laughing. Maybe they hate Gus as much as Cam does. The fire is smaller but still going. The wall with the door in it is the only one standing, scorched black and leaning. He waits until the fishermen get back on their Ski-Doos and leave. It's a good bet someone's already told Gus the news, so he'll have to move fast.

He heads down. In the snow by the cabin, he finds the claw hammer. He takes it and breaks into the boathouse down by the dock. Inside he sees exactly what he hoped for: Gus's other Ski-Doo. He pumps the throttle and presses the starter. Nothing happens, not a sound. He checks the battery — cables are disconnected. He gets them hooked up and the engine turns over, but way too slow. Then he's hearing a snowmobile buzz outside, not close but — Jeez, it's getting louder, coming fast.

Cam peeks out the door. He picks up the hammer and moves quick round the back side of the boathouse. He hears the Ski-Doo roar past the dock and keep going up the slope toward the burning cabin. Through the trees he watches Gus get off the machine and stand there staring, then he goes to the leaning wall and looks through the doorway at the flaring remains. He scrubs a hand over his face, like he's trying to erase what's right there in front of him.

Cam's stands straight as a ramrod behind a cedar trunk. He's afraid to move. Next time he peeks, Gus is by his Ski-Doo with a rifle in his hands. He heads toward the lodge. Then he stops. He turns and looks straight at the boathouse. He starts down the slope.

Cam's frozen, paralyzed. Gus comes past him, not ten feet away, and goes in the boathouse door, and that's when Cam realizes he left the duffle full of cash in there.

For a few seconds, everything's quiet.

Then Gus bellows. "The FUCK."

Gus bursts out the door with the duffle bag in one hand and gun cocked in the other. As he turns toward Cam, Cam charges at him with the hammer swinging. They both go down, tangled up, rolling and sliding down the slope to the dock and the rifle sliding away and Cam still swinging the hammer hard as he can. He sees blood on the snow.

Then it all stops. Gus is on the ground beside him. He's not moving, just moaning. Cam gets onto his feet. He leans over Gus. On the side of his forehead there's a hole punched right through his skull. Blood is pumping out. Cam stares. The hole's deep. Gus's eyeball on the hole side is bulging like it'll pop out.

Cam moves away, but he can't stop looking back at Gus. He picks up the duffle of cash from by the boathouse. Now Gus is trying to get up, but his arms and legs aren't working right. He tries a long time, slipping around on the bloody snow.

Cam stares. Gus is gonna die for sure. How can he not with that hole in his head and the blood pouring out? He's convulsing. Maybe Cam should shoot him right now, like they do to horses. He stares at the rifle lying there on the snow. Then Gus goes completely still, except just one hand twitching. Then that stops. Cam goes over and crouches down next to him. He can see right inside the hole, to the grey matter: Gus's brain. But there's no more Gus in there now.

Cam looks out at the lake. No one's close by that he can see. He has to hide Gus, bury him or — burn him? Or what about down the water hole at the end of the dock? He pulls the hood of Gus's parka up over the mess and ties the hood cords tight, trying not to look at Gus's awful face. Tugging his feet, Cam slides him down to the lake and over the ice to the hole.

Gus goes in fine up to his shoulders, then he jams and his arms flip up. They stay up, like he's waving for help. The parka's all bunched up. Cam looks around the lake. Way out, a fisher is beside his hut with a dog. Cam parks himself in front of Gus and waits till the man goes back inside the hut.

Cam jumps on Gus's shoulders until he's down the hole. He pushes with his feet, soaking his boots, until Gus is shoved along under the ice and doesn't keep bobbing up.

Once the parka's soaked, he'll sink like a stone. The hole will freeze solid and no one will find him till spring or later.

Cam shovels snow with his hands to cover the blood. He takes a bloody animal skin from Gus's butchering place and leaves it on the spot. He tosses the hammer and Gus's red toque into the burning cabin debris.

Gus's Ski-Doo is still puttering away. Cam tosses the cash bag and the rifle into the sled and heads the machine out along the lodge road. Partway back, he realizes he left his snowshoes. Wes won't care, though. Not with all that cash to make up for it.

❧

They've got the bills out on the table, sorted in piles. The total comes to $3,461. Wes is saying the number out loud over and over like he can't believe it.

When Cam came in, he told Wes everything — right in front of Dorie, too. Once he started, he couldn't stop it all pouring out.

Wes was shaking his head after. "A hammer. A friggin' hammer." He was even kind of grinning about it.

They gather up the cash and put it in an old tool box. Wes and Cam each take twenty dollars for their wallets. Now they need a plan. Wes says they get on Gus's machine and go.

"Go where?"

"Just go. Tonight. Late. Across the lake, out the west end. Get a car and drive north, Port Arthur or Kenora or someplace."

"Then what?"

Wes stares at him. "Frig if I know."

33

THERE'S NO MOON AND THE sky is shimmering with a million stars. The lake glows. Cam hangs on, pressed against Wes's back, watching the snow and ice speed past. Now and then he checks on Dorie, behind in the sled with their supplies. They've got clothes and blankets and tools and kitchen stuff from the cabin, along with Gus's rifle and ammo. Wes used to go hunting with his dad, so he knows how to use it.

Gus's bin of fish from the morning run is still in the sled. The fish is frozen now. They could live on it for weeks if they weren't ready to throw up at the idea of more fish. Now they have money for steaks.

Pictures of Gus are still popping up in Cam's head. His greasy hair like there's lard in it. His rotten teeth. His dirty grey beard all brown around his mouth with nicotine. His bloody brain with skull bone crushed into it. Cam doesn't feel bad at all about killing Gus. It was self-defence, but he thinks he might've murdered Gus for real if he had to. He wanted to murder Gramp, too. So it's something that's inside him, just is. He would never kill a good person. But he would've killed Hitler if he could. Lee Harvey Oswald, too.

They're coming up to a shoreline. Wes slows down and they bump up onto a snowmobile path going in through the trees. They pass a shuttered-up cottage and in a while come out to a road, then a paved highway. The ditch is a snowmobile trail. The headlight makes the ditch seem like a snowy tunnel they're endlessly going through.

Cam keeps nodding off, then snaps awake again. They go for ages, it seems. Eventually there's some lights up ahead. Cam sees a neon *MOTEL* sign. Wes stops when they get close. They sit there a minute or two. Cam's about to ask what's up, but then Wes runs the Ski-Doo across the drive and down the trail again on the other side. Now there's some crossroads and a few houses. Then a sign says *Welcome to Elliot Lake.*

Wes knows he decided right about the motel. For a moment all he could think about was a hot shower and a fresh bed. Too risky. He'd like to know if they're in the papers still; could even be on TV, too.

He leaves Cam and Dorie on a side trail just outside town and starts walking in along the highway. Wes remembers Elliot Lake. When his dad got rushed to the hospital their last summer at the cabin, he and his mom stayed in town to be close. All Wes wants from the place now is to buy a decent used car, ditch Gus's snowmobile, and drive as far away as they can.

Takes him a while trudging around the streets to find a used car place. Now he's looking at a Studebaker with *$299* posted on its windshield, next to an auto repair shop. Only two other cars on offer, one a rustbucket Rambler and the other a Ford that looks too much like Wes's. The sun's only just up now but there's a fellow moving around inside the office. Wes goes over and knocks on the window. He's already decided on a fake name for the vehicle registration: Ray Bradbury.

A little later he's driving back to where he left Cam and Dorie. They load their gear into the trunk and leave Gus's beat-up Ski-Doo and frozen fish sitting for whoever wants them. Back on the highway, Wes heads north.

"Crank up the heater, Wes — Dor and I are froze stiff."

"She's cranked."

"It's not blowing too warm."

"You don't like the car I got?"

"It's a real nice car, Wes."

They stop at a roadside place and Wes goes in for fried egg and bacon sandwiches and coffee. They sit in the car and wolf down the food without saying a word. Wes thinks it's about the best meal he's had in months.

"Wes?"

"Yup?"

"Where we going?"

"Dunno. Winnipeg? Regina? Christ, we can go to Vancouver if we want."

"Where we gonna stay?"

"We'll figure that. For now we drive, sleep in the car."

But Cam has an idea. It popped into his head when Wes was buying breakfast and he's been chewing on it along with his egg and bacon. Out on the road every day, there's nowhere to hide. They need a place no one ever comes near. The only place he can think of is Cindy's. Could be vacant. They'd've taken her body away over a month ago now. Nothing to lose by going past the house for a look.

The blacktop is speeding toward Cam, taking them fast in the wrong direction. He has to say it now, before they get so far Wes'll refuse to turn around.

"Wes, you gotta stop. Stop the car."

"What the hell ..."

"STOP THE CAR."

Wes pulls to the side, the tires riding up hard against the banked snow. A truck roars past with its air horn blasting.

"I know where we can go."

Wes just looks at him and waits. Cam stares out the window and talks about driving Cindy home from the laundromat, and how she gave him pie. He leaves out the sex part. Then his trip later to ask her for money. Wes and Dorie don't say a word until he gets to the bloody bathroom.

"She got murdered!" Dorie says all excited.

"No, Dor. She did it. She wanted to die. When I came back to Willard, I phoned a hospital. Didn't say my name or anything, just told them to come get her out of there."

Wes and Dorie are quiet.

"So whatta you say, Wes? Think we can go take a look? Maybe the place is empty."

Wes says, "But she's got family, right? They're gonna come by."

"Don't think she has any family. They're all dead or something. That's why she did it."

Wes turns the car around.

34

WHEN THEY GO BY CINDY'S, they see the drive's been plowed
out and partly drifted in again. Cam can see Cindy's Falcon, still
completely snowed in beside the house. Wes pulls the Ford over a
little bit past the house.

"I'll go knock. I can say we got lost and need directions."

"No one's gonna answer, Wes, I betcha anything."

Cam and Dorie wait in the car. Wes isn't gone too long.

"Place is empty. I knocked front and back. Banged on the windows. Don't see any tracks around."

"Let's go in. Take a look, anyway."

They watch until the highway's clear as far as they can see. Wes
U-turns and guns the car down the long drive. Cam lets them in
the back door with the hidden key. The kitchen smells horrible.
Cam guesses right away it's just rotten potatoes, but he heads to the
bathroom. There's no Cindy in the tub now. The water's drained
but there's still dried blood all over.

Dorie comes up beside him and peers at the mess. "See, I told
you she got murdered."

"Murdered herself, Dor."

They get their supplies inside the house and the rotten potatoes tossed out. The house is chilly but not freezing like outside. Cam and Wes go down to the cellar and stare at the furnace. They try to find a control switch but no luck. Then the furnace comes on by itself.

They find the thermostat in the upstairs hall. Someone put it at fifty degrees. Wes turns it to seventy.

It's lunchtime. Cam opens the fridge. They sit around Cindy's kitchen table, eating Velveeta cheese and Spam and crackers and butter and sweet pickles till they're full up. Then Dorie goes exploring. Wes is getting a worried look.

"Not too sure about this place, Cam."

But all Cam can think is either this place, or driving forever and camping in the car every night with police always on the lookout for them. "See, she had no family, right? No one's come near the place. Why's it sitting here empty for over a month, and everything just like she left it?"

"We don't know. That's just it." Wes goes to the fridge. "Christ, I could use a beer right now, or a shot of whisky more like." He starts opening cupboards. "Bingo!" He takes a bottle down. "Old Niagara Sherry."

Cam gets a thought. He grabs his coat and heads out. He trudges along the snowy drive and waits behind a tree till the highway's clear and he can check the mailbox. Sure enough, the box is crammed full of mail like no one bothered to look since Cindy died. There's magazines and rolled-up papers and letters. He takes it all and heads back to the house.

Wes is fiddling with Cindy's television and getting nothing but static. They go through the newspapers. No mention of them at all. Cam almost feels disappointed, but he knows that's a crazy thought.

"Makes sense," says Wes. "Won't be news till they find us."

Cam spreads the mail out on the kitchen table. There's a hand-addressed envelope with an American stamp on it. Some bills:

a fuel oil company, Algoma Telephone, and two from Ontario Hydro with one stamped in red — *PAST DUE*. There's two from the Dominion Bank. Cam opens them. Wes is across the table, watching him, sipping sherry and ginger ale out of a glass.

"Want some? It's not bad."

"Shouldn't be drinking so early, Wes."

"C'mon. This here is granny stuff."

Cam's looking at Cindy's banking statements: numbers and dates and not much else. There's a few cancelled cheques. Two of them are for $175. Wes reaches and slides the papers across. He looks over the statements and lines up the cheques alongside.

"These are rent. Gotta be. For the house. Dates say first of the month, January and February. Same name, too. We got a land-lord." Wes reads it out: "Edwin B. Hoare." He tips more sherry into his ginger ale. "He'll be wanting a cheque for March. Unless he knows your gal is dead. And then he'd be looking for a new renter."

"Maybe she sent him March rent already."

"Cam, it's real obvious, we gotta skedaddle."

"You wanna live in the car?"

"Yup, live in the car. Friggin' right. I really want that. No, wait, know what I want? I want Edwin B. Hoare to show up and he says he'll call the cops on us and when he's reaching for the phone I grab him and we tie him up and leave him out in the snow till he's froze to death. How's that? Would that be a friggin' plan?"

"Well ..."

"WELL?"

"Well, we already killed three people."

Wes stares at him. "Two. Luke Price was an accident."

"Makes no difference."

Cam sees Wes's eyes kind of freeze, looking at nothing. Then they start moving around. He's watching something inside his head.

"Wes?"

"That church lady, Gurney, she was still alive even after I run her over, what, three or four times?"

"How was she alive?"

"Her face. Her mouth."

"Talking like?"

Wes looks at Cam and moves his mouth:

"Aaa ... aaa ... aaa ..."

"Jeez."

"Yah. Even with her brains out."

"How'd she talk with her brains out?"

"Just part out. So she's saying aaa ... aaaaa ... aaaaaaaa ... Like a baby. Then it stopped. Friggin' weird. It keeps coming into my head."

"Don't be bothered by it, Wes. Gurney and Gus, they were bad people."

"You bothered?"

"I'm not thinking on it much. Some people are better dead — I know that, anyway."

"Yah. And some folks think queers oughta be dead, too."

"What do you mean, Wes?"

"Us. Who else."

"But we're not. That."

"What are we?"

"Doesn't matter what. We're us."

They sit quiet awhile. Dorie's off somewhere talking to herself.

Cam says, "Welp, someone's gotta clean that bathroom. Guess it's me."

"Why bother? We're not staying here."

Cam just heads down the hall.

✼

Wes lies wide awake with the morning light coming in. Cam and Dorie are in Cindy's bed across the hall. Wes's room has a sewing machine and an ironing board and a big old desk with a rolltop. He rolled the top back before he got in bed and found a bunch of homemade jams and pickles. Now he's staring at the rows of Mason jars with little handwritten labels, and he's thinking it's a damn shame they can't stay here awhile and have a decent place to live until — but until what? They got nothing else but until, every single day.

He gets up and has a long piss in the bathroom that Cam's made pretty much spotless. Seems Cam is all set to start a new life here with central heating and frilly curtains and girlie stuff everywhere you look. He's just not thinking straight.

Wes runs the hot water tap in the sink. They got the tank turned on last night, but the water was barely warm by bedtime. Now it's good and hot. Wes strips down and gets the shower going, and once he's in with the steaming water pouring down on his back and shoulders, he actually feels like the world is okay — for a few minutes, anyway. He washes himself all over with Cindy's Ivory soap and scrubs his hair and beard with her shampoo. It feels so friggin' good. Then he's thinking about breakfast.

He remembers seeing a box of Cream of Wheat in the cupboard. He'll have a hot bowlful topped with jam and butter. That's as far ahead as he can think right now.

He goes back to his room. There's Cam in the bed with a big woody tenting up the top sheet. Wes clicks the door shut and climbs in beside him.

When they're done, they lie there quiet. Then they hear the furnace kick on in the cellar and a whispery sound of warm air coming out the vent. They're spooning. Wes is nuzzling the back of Cam's neck, his hand resting along Cam's side, cupping the curve of his hip. He whispers in Cam's ear: "You are the friggin' best."

Cam just nestles himself a little closer to Wes.

"We gotta make it last, Wes."

"Sure will."

"Doesn't matter what folks think. They just don't know."

"That's it. That is exactly it."

"And no more killing."

"Naw. What for?"

Cam makes a big pot of wheat porridge. They open up two jars of jam: raspberry and peach. It starts to snow and before they're finished breakfast there's nothing but solid white outside the kitchen window. They can't eveh see the fir trees in Cindy's yard. It storms like that till past lunchtime, the wind whistling in and making the house creak. Then it turns to freezing rain. By suppertime they still hear it hitting the windows.

❖

Next morning the sun is glaring across acres of untouched snow. Cindy's clothesline is two ice ropes sagging from the pulleys. Wes stares out the front window at the buried Studebaker. He can't even see Cindy's car.

"Guess we're safe for staying longer, Wes."

"How'd you figure that?"

"Need a plow to get in or out."

"Be the landlord driving it."

"Maybe."

Dorie wants to go out and play. They tell her she has to stay in the back, out of sight of the highway. When she gets out she takes a few steps on the ice crust and then crunches through up to her waist. She starts sliding around on her tummy, flapping her arms like a penguin. Wes and Cam can't help laughing.

Later, Wes is in the front room trying to get some news on the TV, or at least a decent picture to help keep Dorie out of trouble. Cam comes in and plunks himself down on the sofa.

"Wes, we gotta have a talk."

"So talk."

"Look, we went through that whole stack of newspapers. No nothing, not about us and not about any human bones down in Bruce County. Like you said, we're not news anymore. Nobody knows except police and no way would police ever look for us here. I say we stay. If the landlord comes by, we say we're cousins of Cindy's, tell him how broke up we are about it. Tell him we wanna rent the place. Give him fake names. We pay him cash, like enough for two or three months. He'd be crazy to say no."

"You got it all worked out."

"Yup, I do. You got another plan?"

"Told you my plan. When he says who the fuck are you, we knock him out and bury him in the snow."

"Or we just leave, if that's what he wants. We pay him our rent time and go. We leave the house real clean and tidy. Just like we're regular folks."

Wes keeps playing with the TV dials, but he's thinking Cam might be right.

35

A COUPLE DAYS LATER, SOMEONE comes and plows the drive. They watch the truck head back down the highway toward Willard. Wes gets his coat on.

"Help me dig the car out, I'm going shopping."

As Wes is about to head out the drive, Cam stops him. He goes inside and opens the overdue electric bill. He puts cash in the envelope and takes it out to Wes.

"You gotta mail this, to pay the hydro."

"Why bother?"

"They'll cut the juice off. You wanna freeze in the dark?"

While Wes is gone, Cam looks over Cindy's mail again. He opens the hand-addressed letter from the States.

Dear Cindy,

We are so sorry to hear about Bill. Thank God he did not suffer long. Came back ok from that mess in Korea and now he's taken from you, what rotten luck for you both. He is in Jesus arms now. Been such a long time since I heard from you and now

your saying your back east. Well I am sending our
condolances now and want you to know our hearts
go out for you. If I heard from you I would of come
up to Kelowna for the funeral.

I do not have the money to help you I will say
that right out. I got laid off two years ago now. Deb
and me we have some health problems too. She goes
in to Phoenix twice a week for the dialysis. I was
driving her most times unless my nerve pain flared
up. Now she takes the bus and stays overnight with
Sue. In a week they are doing my gallbladder, hardly been sleeping with the pain in my gut. People say
its like knives well that's about it, no joke. You can
guess what all this is costing us, all we have now is
my disibility check, about a pile of beans worth so
we are using our savings too.

Sorry to give you the sob story but that is the
truth. You know we would of helped if we could.
Take care and don't let yourself get too down. You
are a strong gal I know that. It all happens for a reason no matter what and if you keep your Faith that
will guide you along on the journey.

Come down for a visit if you get the chance. You
won't get the VIP treatment but it would be good to
see you, been 6 or 7 years anyway, hard to believe.

Love from Chuck and Deb and God Bless

Cam folds the letter back into the envelope. All he can think
is Jesus sure didn't help Cindy. Never did a thing for the Blisses,
either.

• • •

The highway to Willard is clear and dry, not much traffic at all. Outside town there's an OPP car sitting. Wes drives by exactly at the speed limit. At the IGA he fills up the cart with eggs, butter, bread, sausage, hamburger, thick rib-eye steaks for him and Cam, coffee, pancake mix, syrup, peanut butter and chocolate milk and snacks for Dorie, and batteries for the radio — stuff they did without way too long at the cabin. Then straight to the liquor store for a bottle of Crown Royal.

Back out on the highway, he sees the electric bill still sitting on the seat beside him. Well, frig, it can wait. Hydro never shuts off power mid-winter.

Something's rattling under the Studebaker. Then suddenly it gets a lot worse.

Wes stops and takes a look. Tailpipe's dangling about an inch off the road. He ties it up to the bumper with a piece of rope. The muffler's still hanging low, but he'll have to rig that when he gets back.

He's about halfway home and there's another OPP in a different spot. Wes cruises past. He sees the car pull out in his rear-view. The cop keeps his distance for a mile or two, then he pulls up close. Wes keeps going, just moves right a bit like he's giving him room to pass. But sure enough, the flashing lights come on and the cop's waving him over.

The officer's paunchy and red-faced. "I'll need licence, registration, and insurance, sir."

Wes pops the glovebox. He can't show his driver's licence — not a chance. He hands the cop the registration slip. "Picking up the insurance papers tomorrow, officer."

"Your licence, sir."

"Well, I'm feeling kind of stupid — left my wallet at home."

"This your vehicle?"

"Yessir, it is. That's my name there, Ray Bradbury."

The cop goes behind the car and checks the plate against the registration, then he's back with his mirror sunglasses staring at Wes.

"Mr. Bradbury, you and your vehicle are right now in violation of three or four laws. Number one, no licence; number two, this slip here is expired. You need a DOT card within four days of purchase, with your home address — not a P.O. box, you aware of that?"

"Yessir, I am. We're just new here in this area. I'll get it all straightened out right away, first thing tomorrow."

The cop takes off his sunglasses. His eyes move around the interior of the car.

"You seem a little anxious, sir."

"Just gotta get home, that's all."

"Where's that, your postbox in Thessalon?"

"No, sir, just, uh, local here, for the winter."

The cop steps back. "Sir, I will ask you to step out of the car."

"What for?"

"Out. Now."

"But I haven't done anything."

The officer grabs the door handle. Wes rams the car in gear and floors the accelerator. In his rear-view, he sees the cop on the ground. Wes gears up and pushes pedal to the metal. The Studebaker roars and shudders, then there's a bang and the muffler is skidding along the pavement behind him. Way back, he sees the cop stumbling to his car. Wes tears down the highway like some crazy hot rodder, the speedometer creeping up to seventy miles an hour, then almost eighty, but not quite. Not enough to outrun a cop car. He sees the flashing lights far behind him just as he goes into a curve and brakes too late and the car spins out and hits the ditch sideways and rolls.

Wes is out in the snow, staring at a spinning tire. He gets on his feet and runs for the woods above the ditch, straight into a barbed-wire fence, but he's up and over and keeps going in through the trees. He's tasting blood in his mouth. He's got a horrible pain in his left shoulder. He keeps going, slogging through the snow, stumbling and falling and up again, going and going through the trees till he comes to a clearing and collapses. His shoulder is agony. He lies there listening to cop sirens. He's got to keep moving.

Wes is gone way too long for shopping. Cam guesses he's drinking in the legion hall. Then it's dark and he's still not back. Cam spends the whole night crazy with worry. He tries to get some news in the morning but the TV's useless. Dorie stops asking questions and just stays away from him.

Maybe he can get Cindy's car going? It's pretty mild weather today. Might start on the first go if he pumps it. He digs out the snow-heaped Falcon and yanks open the driver's door. The dome light is dead. He hits the horn button and flicks the headlights: nothing. Coming back to the porch, he sees something dark moving out in the field to the east. Then he hears his name. Friggin' Jesus, it's Wes.

Back in the house, Wes starts shaking, like outside he was so frozen he couldn't even do that. He has cuts on his hands and forehead and crusty blood in his beard. Cam knows to thaw him out slow. He helps Wes to the kitchen and gives him sips of warm coffee. He gets a cloth to wash his bloody face. He asks what happened, but all Wes says is "car crash." Then he tells Cam how to pop his dislocated shoulder back in, the way his dad used to do. He yowls when the bones clap together again. He's still shaking, his whole body. He goes still a little while and then it starts again.

Wes starts talking about the OPP stop, why he crashed.

"Never showed my licence. All they got is a fake name and a P.O. box."

• • •

It starts snowing again. Keeps up all afternoon and right through suppertime. When it gets dark, they decide they can turn the lights on only in the kitchen — it's the one window that can't be seen from the highway. Cam makes a supper of rice, canned peas, and ketchup. He bakes it in a casserole dish. It comes out burnt on top and tastes pretty bad. Dorie takes two bites and calls it pukey and starts getting real lippy. Wes finally reaches out and slaps her.

"Wes! Jesus …"

Wes gets out of his chair and pulls Dorie off hers and drags her to the kitchen door. "Goddamn sick of you, Dor. OUT. GO LIE DOWN."

Dorie's so surprised she doesn't even cry, just disappears down the hall. Wes comes back and shovels the food into his mouth.

"Kid's a friggin' ingrate — sick to death of it. Nothing wrong with this food, Cam." He scoops more onto his plate.

Cam goes to find Dorie. She's crying on the bed.

"Wes didn't mean that, Dor. He's just —"

"I hate him. I hate this place. I WANNA GO HOME."

Cam stays with her until the crying stops. Back in the kitchen, he makes some jam on crackers for her. Wes has his head in his hands.

"You gotta go and apologize, Wes."

"Yup, I will."

"Wes, listen, we should just go. We got Cindy's car — all we need is a battery. I could steal one. That garage a couple miles down the highway."

"You know how much a car battery weighs?"

"Think I can't handle it?"

"I know it. Plus everyone driving past sees you lugging it like a goddamn thief, including the cops."

36

WES HASN'T SLEPT A WINK. His shoulder is throbbing. His mind is stuck on every detail of the OPP stop and what the cop said to him, what he might've done instead of taking off like a for-real criminal. But that's what he is.

After supper he went and apologized to Dorie. He said all the troubles made the three of them kind of nutty and he never meant to smack her like that, said he won't ever do it again, promise and cross his heart. He kissed her forehead. Dorie stared up at him with the pink bedspread pulled up tight to her chin. She wasn't crying, but she looked at him like he was a stranger.

Alone in bed now, thinking about Dorie and Cam, Wes can actually feel his heart paining him. He's the only one to keep them safe, and he's not coming through. He finally dozes. Doesn't know if he's asleep or awake, crazy stuff racing through his mind.

Cam's lying awake, thinking there must be some way he could start the Falcon. Maybe rig a wire from the furnace thermostat?

It's likely twelve volts, or close to it, but he'd need forty or fifty feet of wire. He gets up and searches the basement — no luck. Back upstairs, morning light is coming in. He stands in the front room, staring out the window to the highway. A few cars and trucks go by, then a black-and-white OPP car. It zooms straight past the driveway and disappears to the east.

To help calm himself, Cam makes a big batch of porridge and brews up the last of Cindy's coffee. He hears Wes moving around.

Then he's calling, "Cam! Someone's plowing the drive."

They watch, peeking out the front window. Looks like the same truck as last time. When it finishes by the house, the driver gets out and comes right up to the porch. They back away out of sight. They can hear him tugging open the screen door. Then the inside door opens. The driver's in the front hall, stamping snow off his boots. Then he comes round the corner and his jaw drops.

"What the hell ...?"

They tackle him. He fights awhile, but he's old and not too big. They get him flat on his back, Cam holding his legs and Wes pinning his arms.

Dorie's watching from down the hall. "Are you an OPP?"

The man twists his neck and stares at Dorie. When he looks back at Cam, his eyes are wild.

"Oh my God, don't kill me. Please."

Wes says, "You think we're killers?"

"You ... that girl. On the radio, the Bliss Gang."

"The Bliss Gang? What the hell's that?"

"Just let me go. I won't say a word. Take the truck. Please don't hurt me. Please."

Cam says, "We're not like that. A gang. You think we just go round and murder folks?"

"No. I don't think that. Take the truck and leave me here, just leave me." The man's shaking. Then he's shouting. "PLEASE ... PLEASE ..."

"Cam, go get some rope."

They take him to the basement and tie him to a chair. They rope him and the chair to a steel support post. He's not saying a word now, just breathing hard with his eyes closed.

When they're upstairs, he starts shouting again. Wes swears and goes down the hall. When he comes back, he's got the rifle.

"Won't shoot him, just gonna shut him up."

Whatever Wes does downstairs, it works. He comes up and lays the gun on the kitchen table. Cam stares at it. The barrel's glossy black. The butt end is scarred wood. Cam looks up and Wes is staring right into his eyes.

"The man's right. Killers."

"Put it away."

"Gotta load it."

"So load it. Take it. Take it outta here."

The porridge is burnt to the bottom of the pot. Wes says they have to eat it, keep their strength up. Dorie spoons out half a jarful of jam on hers and Cam just watches, thinking why say anything, why does it even matter now.

Wes is watching Dorie too, then he says, "Dorie, I'm gonna tell you something. Put your spoon down. Look at me."

Dorie does what she's told.

"We love you, Dor. Don't say it too much but it's the truth. Right, Cam?"

"Sure is."

"And we're gonna keep you safe. But we need your help, to remember your promise. Not to say anything about us, not to anyone. Not about the church lady or about Gramp or Luke Price. Not about the cabin or Scotch Lake. Or Gus. Not even if police are asking."

"Are the OPPs coming?"

"They might. So it's like they say on TV. You tell them you're not gonna talk. You say, 'I have the right to remain silent.' Can you say that? Say it."

"I have the right to remain silent."

"Good. That's all you need to say, if the police or anyone ever starts asking questions. Okay?"

"Yip."

"Good girl. Now eat your porridge."

They decide to leave the man in the basement, take the truck, and head west. They can ditch it before anyone's on the lookout for it and get another car. By tomorrow they'll be in Winnipeg.

Wes goes back to the basement. "You Edwin Hoare?"

"I'm his brother."

"When's he gonna miss you?"

"Not him who's gonna miss me. It's my wife'll miss me."

"Well, someone'll come find you, then. We're outta here. We are not what you said. That gang. We're just some folks down on our luck. Used your house a few days. Here's something for your trouble."

He shoves a couple twenties in the man's coat pocket.

Wes is stowing their gear in the truck when he sees the black-and-white cars rolling to a stop on the highway. OPP, three of them, blocking the drive. He doesn't even need to think. He's back in the house and down the stairs to the basement with a kitchen knife in one hand and the rifle in the other. He cuts their prisoner free but leaves his hands tied.

He hustles him up and out the front door, shouting at Cam to get himself and Dorie in the truck with the cash box. He stands the man up in the middle of the driveway with the rifle held on him. He watches the cops slinking out of their cruisers. They crouch behind the cars with their guns aimed. Wes shouts down the drive. He tells the cops they have five minutes to let them pass.

"FIVE MINUTES."

Cam gets Dorie in the truck. She doesn't make a sound, just sits with her eyes pressed shut. He starts the engine.

A voice comes from the cop cars, a megaphone. It says to drop the gun. It says co-operate and no one will get hurt. Cam watches Wes point the rifle at the sky. He fires it once. The man crumples, but Wes wrestles him up again.

The man breaks away. He runs a few steps and goes down flat in the snow and then the cops are firing, they're firing at Wes and Wes's head snaps back, blood is flying in the air and Wes is down, then it's quiet, completely quiet, but now someone is screaming, so loud, and Cam's out of the truck, falling, crawling to Wes, and Cam knows it's himself who's screaming. He's holding Wes, watching the blood pour out of him. Wes's eyes are on Cam's face.

THE OPP STATION SMELLS LIKE coffee and cigarettes. Dorie's on a hard chair beside a big wooden desk. The police lady smiles at her.

"Can you tell me your complete name, Dorie?"

"Dorothy."

"Dorothy who?"

"Nothing."

"You can tell me — it's all right."

"Is Wes gonna die?"

"No. He will be okay. Is Wes Cody your uncle, Dorie?"

"Dunno. He's Wes."

"And what is Cam? Cousin? Brother?"

"Cousin."

"Tell me about the farm, Dorie. What happened there?"

"Nothing. We lived there."

"But we know something happened. That's why they took you away. That's why Wes got shot. You can help us."

"Nothing happened. I don't need to tell. I have the right to remain silent. I wanna see Cam and Wes. Why can't I see them?"

Dorie starts crying.

"You can see them if you help us. Cam and Wes did bad things. People got hurt. We found their bones at the farm. Someone burned them. You need to tell us about it."

"NO I DON'T."

Dorie gets off the chair and runs out of the office door and past a bunch of desks and people until hands grab her and lift her up and she's looking right in the big face of a man with a moustache.

"Where you going, little lady?"

The man plunks her down on another hard chair.

�֍

The police are eating takeout hamburgers at their desks. Cam can smell the food from his cell. They offered to get a burger for him, but he's not hungry.

After lunch, two cops take Cam to a room. They sit him down at a bare table and show him a picture of Luke Price. They say they know he came to the farm. They tell him the exact date and time. Cam tells them Luke came and went, that's all. Haven't seen him since. They keep firing questions at him but Cam just folds his arms and clams up. One cop is quiet and reasonable, but the other one raises his voice, then he pounds the table and leaves the room. Then the nicer cop says Cam could just be honest with them, come clean, and he'll feel better and won't have to go to jail. He tells Cam they can make a deal because he's younger than Wes. He says Cam has a right to a lawyer. He slides a phone across the table.

"Do you have anyone you can call, tell them your situation?"

Cam doesn't know what to say. Who can he call? There's no one. He just hopes they told him the truth about Wes, that he'll be okay once they patch him up. In his mind he sees Wes's face, his cheek ripped apart, smashed teeth, blood soaking his parka.

Now Cam's in a cell. He heard Dorie shouting somewhere down the other end of the station. He's not even surprised that his cell looks so much like the ones on TV. Same iron bars, same little bed and nothing else.

He wishes they would let Dorie be with him. He wishes he could pee, but they're making him wait.

"Hello? Hello? I need to pee. I NEED TO USE THE TOILET."

They ignore him.

A bit later the nicer cop, Officer Deakin, comes and takes him down the hall to a bathroom. Then they go to the interrogation room again. Deakin sits opposite Cam. He's got a notepad and pencil. His face is smooth and clean-shaven. He's younger than the others.

"Cam, honestly, you should just relax and not worry too much. We're on your side. But I do have to let you in on something. Our boys down in Walkerton were talking to folks who know you and your family, people who knew your grandparents and so on. They said a thing about you and Wes."

"Who said?"

"Well, more than one. We have more than one source. They said you fellows, you and Wes, had indecent relations. Homo is what I'm saying."

"They're a buncha liars."

"Who is?"

"McKicrans, all of them. Doug Johnstone, too."

"Another thing, Cam, is that we heard about you and your grandfather, and you and Luke Price. And the burning. And our sources are good, it matches up with what we found, what the forensic lab says, about the bones."

"What bones?"

"You tell me. Tell me why you killed and burned your grandfather. Tell me why you killed Dorothy Price's father and burnt him, too. A helpless old man and a little girl's father. To be honest with you, we think Wes did it, and you went along because he made you. He's the one responsible. You can tell us that. You don't need to protect him. You can get it off your conscience. Don't you want that? You're free from Wes now. We understand how it happened. We know about Miss Gurney, too, how she went to see you fellows about Dorothy and that was the end of her. If you tell us where her body is, then her family at least can have a proper Christian burial. I think she knew about you and Wes, too. Didn't she? How Wes forced his perversions on you. Well, that's over now. You can have a decent and normal life again."

The cop is looking at Cam with sad eyes, like he cares.

"Nothing to say?"

"You got it wrong. You got it so wrong I can't even …"

"Do you believe in God, Cam? Do you believe human life is sacred?"

"There's no God."

"Well. You're Godless, then."

"Yep. You're Godless, too."

"No. God's laws are the laws of this land. Murder is the worst crime, the worst sin. Homosexuality is a sin too, and also a crime. You might feel loyal to Wes, but deep down you know he's in the wrong. He is a dangerous and degenerate man. You have to face that." Deakin stands up. "Can I get you something? A Coke? A root beer?"

"You don't know anything. You're the one telling lies, making stuff up."

"I understand. You need some thinking time."

The cop puts his hand on Cam's shoulder and holds it there, looking at Cam with his sad and reasonable face. He takes a phone book out of a drawer and puts it beside the phone. He leaves Cam in the interrogation room. It's got a big mirror on one wall and Cam knows it's gotta be a two-way. He stares at the mirror, at his own face that's got cop faces right there behind the glass, watching him. He wants to scream at them to go to hell and never come back. Instead he opens the phone book and looks in the yellow pages for lawyers.

38

THE PAIN IN WES'S FACE and head and shoulder is terrible. For days it seemed he was so doped up he didn't know if he was awake or dreaming. Sometimes he'd be in his hospital bed with nurses around and a cop sitting by his door, sometimes at the farm or driving or at the cabin with Cam and Dorie. Or lying in the snow with Cam there, holding him.

It hurts to move his mouth. His voice is all slurry when he asks the nurses where Cam and Dorie are, if they're okay. They say the police have to answer those questions. He touches his face and they tell him not to, but he felt the bandages. His face on one side is numb and heavy. Pains shoot up through his skull and down his neck and arm. The nurses give him pain pills, but it doesn't help much. They said one bullet broke his jaw and they took another one out of his left shoulder. He's lucky to be alive.

The cop outside the door comes and goes but he's never gone for long. Nurses say he never leaves the floor. He keeps looking in to make sure Wes didn't disappear or jump out the window. Do they think he's friggin' Houdini?

One day there's two guys in suits and ties beside his bed. They stand there with a nurse, all three of them looking at Wes like he's a problem they gotta solve.

"Mr. Cody, we need to talk."

"Nope, I don't need to."

"Let's give it a try."

"I wanna know if Cam and Dorie are okay."

"Cameron Bliss is in custody. He's fine — so is the girl."

They show Wes a photo of Luke Price.

"Who's this? Ever seen him?"

Wes squints. "Looks like that movie star fella."

"Think harder."

"Paul Newman?"

"You're related to him."

"Can't see too clear."

"We know you killed him, Cody."

Wes starts moaning. He says he needs a pain pill. He closes his eyes and grimaces like he's in agony.

The cops leave. Wes tells himself he won't crack no matter what. How much could they know? Not much about Gurney. And all they got otherwise is bones and ashes.

Later the nurse says he got a phone call, from a lawyer.

"I never called a lawyer."

"He wants you to call him back."

So Wes talks to the lawyer. He learns that Cam already talked to him. He's from Sudbury and his name is Morris something. He says Cam is in an OPP holding cell and Dorie is now with the local Children's Aid. He tells Wes to say nothing to the cops. He'll come by the hospital in a day or two.

✳

The hospital puts Wes in a small room with a desk. They wanted to take him in a wheelchair, but he refused. He's not planning to be an invalid.

The nurse leaves him a pain pill and a paper cup of juice. He sits waiting for the lawyer, looking around at medical posters on the walls, pictures of people's insides. He's already had his hospital breakfast: porridge and lukewarm scrambled eggs. He can't have toast or anything that needs chewing. He spooned bits of egg into his mouth and took sips of milky tea to wash it down.

The door opens.

"Wesley Cody?"

"Just Wes, if you don't mind."

His voice is a croak. He has to talk without hardly moving his jaw.

"Wes, I'm Morris Geller, your attorney."

"How much you gonna cost?"

Geller smiles. "We'll work that out."

"Cops took our money — three thousand cash."

"It's still your money, until they put theft on the charge sheet."

Geller closes the door and claps his briefcase down on the desk. He's got it open before he's even sitting down. He pulls out some forms, explains a bunch of stuff, and tells Wes to sign in two places.

Wes scans the papers. "Says five hundred dollars here."

"We can't talk without a retainer. The OPP can take it from your cash and you'll get a receipt. We will bill you as the case develops."

Wes signs the papers.

"Good. Thank you for your trust. I spoke with your cousin in person yesterday, also with the OPP investigator. They haven't filed all charges yet, but it's a matter of a day or two. Bad news first: Convictions are certain for the incidents at the house preceding your arrest. It's your word against that of the hostage and six officers."

"Feel bad about that old fella."

"I'm glad you didn't shoot him. Now, for the alleged murders: they have evidence, circumstantial mostly and highly challenge-able, pointing to your possible involvement in three deaths."

"Three?"

"Three. Yes. Do you have a different, um, figure?"

"Who we talking about?"

"Samuel Bliss, Luke Price, Beulah Gurney."

"Never killed Sam — Luke either."

"Nor Beulah Gurney, not by the evidence."

"Okay."

"What have you said to the police so far?"

"Nothing. Zero."

"Your cousin told them that Luke Price came to your house last August, looking to see Dorothy."

"He said that?"

"Did it happen?"

"Yup, it did."

"That's all that Cam has told them, apparently, but it's a pivotal issue. Unfortunately, it's an admission that Price was at your farm just before he went missing. And the bones, of course, found later on your land. But we will challenge the dental evidence, and in any case it's completely irrelevant vis-à-vis cause of death. As to your grandfather, Cameron's I mean, they seem to have a witness, a neighbour."

"He's a liar."

"Who is?"

"Kyle McKieran. He knocked up Dorie, too."

"He — raped Dorothy?"

"Took her in his barn and messed with her. She'll tell you."

"All right, that could help."

"You gonna get us off?"

"On the murder charges, we have an excellent shot."

"You got to keep Cam out of jail. He could not handle it. No one else to take care of Dorie, either."

"Dorie, I'm afraid, will go to foster care. I don't see any other outcome. As for Cam, being a minor, that already makes you the culpable one. We'll see what they have."

"Cam'll be an adult soon. Dorie doesn't need friggin' foster care."

"Mr. Cody, the OPP considers your history with Cam and Dorie to be of special interest. The Crown will follow suit. They want a conviction and this offers the path of least resistance, because of your alleged — I say alleged — relations with Cam."

"Relations? We're cousins."

"There's a question of homosexual activity. It boosts the claim that Cam is a victim and that you are culpable. Basically, it's their best bet to bias the jury against you and help ensure they convict. But acquittal all round is what we want, obviously."

"We're not homo."

"I'm sure you're not. But a jury, given the expected testimony, may think otherwise."

"Well, fuck them right up the wazoo is what I say."

"Mr. Cody, you must not say that, or anything similar, even behind closed doors. Now. The charges. They will most likely be murder first or second degree for the two men. As for the woman, she is officially missing. They do not have a body. It seems they found an amount of body matter, unburnt in this case, on your land, but I doubt they can match it to an individual."

"Body matter ... like how much?"

"We may not learn that until the trial."

"Couldn't be much."

"You wouldn't know. You don't know."

"You're telling me I don't know?"

"That's why you're paying me."

"So ..."

"So, when you've had time to recollect, let me know why you have no idea what happened to Beulah Gurney. Maybe you were not there that day, that time."

Wes stares. He's seeing what he did. That day. "Maybe if it was an accident or something …"

"That's an admission."

"I could do a little time …"

"What would a little time be? Eternity? They still hang men in this country. We start from innocence." Geller stands. "I'll be back soon. Don't share anything with anyone, nurses, whoever."

"Can I talk to Cam?"

"You can't. It may be a few months before you see Cam."

"Months?"

"I'm sorry."

"You're friggin' sorry? What the hell …"

"Mr. Cody, Wes, it is absolutely crucial that you control yourself. No anger, no profanity. Not here, not to the police, and not to me if you can help it."

Wes mumbles, "Yes, sir."

Geller packs up his briefcase. He pauses, looking Wes in the eye. "I've never had a client hanged. The worst I see, I won't soft-pedal it, they could give you life, so, twenty-five years max. A bit less if you behave, or find Jesus."

"Haven't found him yet."

"That would be two of us." Geller turns before he goes out. "Don't phone me. We talk only in this room."

THERE ARE FOUR HOLDING CELLS in the Espanola OPP detachment. Cam's been the only one locked up for the past week almost, except for a couple drunks one night who stank the whole place up. Smelled like Gramp.

A woman comes from Children's Aid. She talks to Cam sitting on a chair outside his cell. She's younger and way nicer than the Gurneys but she says he can't see Dorie again. They've put her in a special home in Espanola, just temporary, until she can go to foster care in Bruce County.

"It's clear that she has never had a proper home, a decent child-hood. You may feel responsible for her, but that's hardly enough to overcome the harm, the harm that you too have experienced, from Mr. Cody and —"

"Wes never harmed me. Gramp did."

"Well, we can't change any of it, but we can help Dorothy. She is out of your care now."

Cam tries to keep his face normal but tears start running down his cheeks. The woman watches him like she's seen this a million times before. She takes a little pack of tissues out of her purse and hands it to him through the bars.

Then he thinks of Uncle Earl. He could take care of Dorie, maybe. Cam tells the woman about him, but she doesn't look too interested. Earl is a bachelor and lives in Toronto. Cam was at his apartment one time. Uncle Earl was nothing like Gramp except he did drink a bit, but he wasn't mean.

Now Cam is on the phone. He's alone in the interrogation room but he figures Officer Deakin is out there, listening in on the call. The operator says she has found an E. Bliss on Dovercourt Road in Toronto.

"That's him!"

There's only two rings and then a man says hello.

"Uncle Earl? It's Cam here, Cam Bliss."

"Jesus Murphy."

"Yep, it's me."

"You killed Sam, murdered him, you and Wes Cody."

"We didn't — he died from drink."

"It's in the papers, killed him and Luke Price too, burnt them, oh my Lord ..."

"We never did."

"Why are you calling me? Where are you?"

"Police station. We got a lawyer."

"Do not call me again. I can't help you."

The phone goes dead.

❊

A few days later, the lawyer comes back. He says Cam's lucky he's still seventeen. The worst he might get is a year or so in reformatory. His only charge is desecration of human remains.

"What about Wes?"

"Murder on three counts."

"He never killed anyone."

"We have a strong case. But juries will disregard reasonable doubt if they dislike a defendant. I'm afraid a guilty verdict on just one charge could put Wes away twenty years or more. Fortunately, he's still young."

"But he'll be an old man when …"

"Fifty, thereabouts. Not quite an old man."

When the lawyer goes, Cam curls up on his hard bed with his face to the wall, and the tears start again.

Next time Geller comes by, he says he got bail for Cam. Cam walks out of the police station with him. It's drizzly outside and the snow's turning to slop. They get into a big Buick with leather seats. Geller doesn't start the car. He just sits looking at Cam.

"Cam, what happened to Luke?"

"He got sick. He came and tried to take Dorie. He got in a fight with Wes and then he sicked up and died on us."

"Did you or Wes kill your grandfather, or help him along to it, to dying?"

"Never did. We took care of him. He drank himself dead."

"And what happened to Miss Gurney?"

"Dunno."

"Was she at the farm that day, before you boys took off?"

"What did Wes say?"

"What do you say?"

"Well, she was there. She talked about taking Dorie. Then she left. That's all."

"All right, then. This is your testimony when they call you at Wes's trial. Everything you just said. Stick to it. I'll help you to remember."

Geller starts the car.

"Where you taking me?"

"Sudbury. You're set up with room and board. That's till they move you and Wes down for trial in Guelph. Any attempt to leave the property unescorted, they will put you right back in lock-up and you'll stay there till trial. Okay?"

"Guess so."

"You'll find other young guys in the house — a few bad eggs, likely. Best to keep to yourself if you can. If you like I can get you some books. They don't allow TV."

"Can I see Dorie?"

"They don't think you're a suitable influence for Dorie."

"I'm the only one she's got."

"I wish I could change things, Cam. I'm sorry."

"When can I see Wes?"

"At trial. Three or four months, if we're lucky."

Geller starts the car and they head out of the OPP lot with the wipers slapping.

"Can I go back to the farm?"

"Well, it's Bliss land, and you're a Bliss. You're free to go home if you're acquitted, or when your time is done, if there's no challenge to the land title."

"Maybe I'll find Gramp's will."

"That could help, or not. He may have left the farm to someone else."

"Like Uncle Earl."

"Are your parents alive?"

"Dunno. Don't care, either."

"If you do find a will, I should be the first to see it."

"I'm not gonna even look for it."

"That might be the best approach." Geller gives him a wink.

the
bliss house

40

HERE COMES DOUG JOHNSTONE'S BOY, out plowing the north field at the Bliss place on a fine spring morning. Like always, Rob slows the tractor a little when he goes past the burning spot. Every time, he can see those human bones in his head, just the way his dad described them. Sometimes he looks up toward the house and his mind starts with all the weird stuff that must've been going on in there for a hundred years or more. Perversions and molestations and kids brought up like animals and likely other murdered folks too that they never found. Cam's in there by himself now, but Wes Cody's still locked up. They say Cam's down to Kingston Pen regular to visit. Rob knows there's lots of pervs in the prisons. If Wes ever gets outta jail, they might even be living their homo lives up here again. Long as they keep to themselves.

As Cam picks up his razor in the bathroom, he glances out the window. That'd be Doug's boy out there on the tractor. Doug has his sons doing the field work these days. Cam hasn't seen Doug in ages. The co-op office does the lease negotiating now. Every November a letter comes and Cam signs the papers and sends them back, and the money keeps coming in.

He stares at his shave-creamed face in the mirror. He still looks like a kid, really. That's what he thinks, anyway. Still has the same hair on top and lots of it. But a more manly beard now, for sure. He shaves it every day with the old Schick and he will so long as the Rexall in town still sells the blades.

When he's had breakfast, he sits down to write his letter to Wes. Now and then they write to each other and exchange the letters when Cam visits. The visitor room is no place for a decent conversation. In the letters they can say whatever they want. Cam has to hand the unsealed envelope to a guard. He opens it up and looks it over and a sniffer dog right there checks it for drugs. Could be LSD in the paper. If the guard reads some of it, well, why would it matter? Wes isn't the only guy in jail with someone on the outside.

Cam'll get up at 5:00 a.m. tomorrow and drive down to Kingston, same as most Sundays. Be there before lunch. He tries never to miss a week, even if they get mad at each other about some dumb thing — always feels worse if he stays home. It's been rough for Wes in there with the hardened criminals. He learned not to mix too much.

Dorie came along a few times, on holidays or whatever, once she was old enough. Then she got married to Tim Boyle and now they got a baby on the way. She never comes to Kingston anymore. Tim doesn't like her to and Cam kind of understands that.

He always brings Wes a burger and large fries. The guards are picky about what kind of food they let in, but McDonald's is okay. They just check it out at the entrance for contraband.

He wanted to bring Wes a Walkman radio, but they don't allow them. He got one anyhow and Wes will get it soon enough. When he's back home. When he's free.

Cam's heart flips every time he pictures it, turning in from the road and coming up the drive with Wes. And Wes getting out of the car and looking around at the place, like he's in a dream, and Cam watching him. The same Wes he's seen only behind glass in the horrible visitor room at Kingston Pen. For eighteen years. But now it'll be over. It will for real be over, all of it, in just one week and four days.

He wipes the flecks of foam from his clean-shaven face and gives himself a once-over. Still hasn't got wrinkles at all except for some crinkly parts at the corners of his eyes. How can he be turning thirty-six next month?

❖

So Dorie's a Boyle now. Tim wants her to quit her morning job at the old folks' home and come work for his dad at the hardware. She said she might. She lets Tim call her Dot. If she's ever out to the farm, Cam still calls her Dorie, like she's still the kid. A few years ago she found her little-kid clothes still in the dresser drawer in the bedroom she shared with Cam. Cam keeps the house the same — same furniture and same Moffat stove and same pots hanging from the pegboard. He even uses the wood stove to heat the place in winter.

Dorie comes by the farm now and then, sometimes with Tim too, but she hasn't slept in the Bliss house since the day they became fugitives from the law and drove away to the north woods. She can hardly believe all of that really happened. Cam said she and Tim could maybe come up to Scotch Lake with him and Wes sometime, once Wes is home. What a loony idea. Why would she wanna see that place again?

Dorie and Tim rent an apartment in town from June and Kurt Schwartz, her former foster parents. She can walk to her job in the mornings at the Geri-Care. Tim's religious, so now Dorie's involved with the Anglican Church Women at St. John's. The people are nice. The thing is, some of them are not so easygoing about homosexuals. Plus there's been all the gossip and outright lies people say about Wes and Cam. Folks say Wes killed Gramp and Beulah Gurney too, even though no one ever found her. And Luke Price, of course, the murder they locked him up for, because Doug Johnstone found his teeth.

Dorie saw what happened with Luke Price. It was a fight, not a murder. She wonders sometimes what her real father was like. She wonders what her life might have been like if none of the bad stuff had happened. But her foster parents were good people. She and Tim see them now and then for Sunday dinner. She used to go out to the farm for dinners too, once in a while, until she married Tim. But Cam will have Wes soon to eat dinners with, and she's not keen to see Wes that much. He's like a stranger.

In her own mind, she thinks Wes probably murdered Miss Gurney. Why else did he have blood all over him that day? But she'd never say that to anyone.

✻

Wes stares at his foamed-up face in the polished steel mirror. He takes the first swipe with the razor. He shaves with special care over the old scars from the police bullets. He still figures they were aiming to kill him. Just dumb luck that he was knocked down and only wounded by the first shots. He sometimes thinks he'd have been okay with death coming at that moment. Cam would've got over it and had a better life, maybe. Or maybe not.

Anyhow, they still got each other and that's good. Hasn't been easy, but just seeing Cam's face, his smile, and talking regular, even through glass — well, it's kept him going through all the shit in this damn place.

The guard will take the razor back in a few minutes — as if Wes is gonna do anything stupid with a blade on today of all days,

the day he steps out through the gates. He'll never see the inside
of a goddamn cell again. Eighteen years. Wes kept to himself in
the Pen. Cam brought him books and he actually started reading
some, depending. Parole board said he was a model prisoner and
showed remorse for his crime. Wes even made himself cry for the
pastor once or twice. Only got in one real knock-down fight the
whole time and only because of a jerk-off who said "faggot" to him
one time too many. The guy was a faggot himself.

He's got about six hundred of his own money coming to him
with his personal kit and the jeans and shirt and shoes Cam
brought in for him a couple weeks ago. Bastards wouldn't even let
him try the stuff on for size.

So now he's in a little room in a part of the Pen he's never seen,
with a guard he's never seen either standing in the doorway, smok-
ing and smirking at him while he gets himself into a pair of jeans
a little too tight in the waist. The shoes are white-and-blue runners
straight out of the box and they fit just fine. He walks in a circle
around the room and then stands at the little window, looking out
at a parking lot and trees and, beyond that, Lake Ontario glinting
in the sun.

"How's the world look?"

Wes turns around. The guard's still smirking at him but that's
okay. Everything's okay.

"You gonna stay on the straight?"

"Think I wanna come back here?"

"Wouldn't be the first. Someone picking you up?"

"My best buddy. Taking me home."

Wes is smiling. Feels like it could split his face. He's smiling at
a prison guard.

"Well, come on, then. Get your kit and put your X on paper
and you're a free man."

"You boys are gonna miss me."

"Like a fuckin' toothache."

*

Cam doesn't sleep much. The butterflies just won't let up in his stomach. He's up and dressed by four. He eats a little breakfast. He's got food in for a homecoming dinner. The sheets and towels are all fresh washed. He even did some painting to spruce the place up a little.

Wes gets out at 1:00 p.m. It's still way too early to leave. Cam sits on the porch with a coffee. The day will be warm, he knows by the smell in the air. Sky's just getting pink over the McKierans' house. Except the McKierans are long gone and the house has town folks in it now. They live in Kitchener and come up on weekends.

What's it gonna be like? Wes in the house every day. His actual real self there. Here. Eating together. Sleeping together? They hardly ever did that. Most times they were in a bed together was sex time. He still wants Wes that way, still feels it when he visits. Wes is forty-six now, but he's been keeping fit, jogging and lifting weights in the Pen. He said Cam oughta try it.

Cam's been working at the Walkerton Library, for years now, just in the afternoons from three to six, sorting and shelving books. Pays almost nothing but that's not why he does it. He doesn't need extra money. Getting out is the main thing. Being with people sometimes.

The new head librarian, Mr. Evelyn, is gay, not that anyone ever says a word about it. He lives with his friend Aaron in a farm-house out near Paisley. Paul and Aaron have had Cam out there a few times. No hanky-panky at all. Mostly it's about drinking wine and eating. They had a big outdoor dinner in the summer at a long table. Must have been twenty or more library types and city people. Cam drank three glasses of wine — most he ever drunk in his life.

Paul and Aaron are what you'd call fascinated with the murder story. After a few drinks they start with the questions. Of course

Cam just lies about Miss Gurney, same as Wes does — says she came to the farm and then went away, like usual. Because as far as anyone knows she's still a missing person. Up there in the trunk of her sunken Merc. He feels bad about her family, but obviously not bad enough to ever rat on Wes.

Cam makes sure people know they didn't kill Gramp. Burnt him, yes. And he tells anyone who wants to listen that Luke Price was just a horrible accident. No one knows about Gus. No one's ever mentioned him, not OPP or anybody. Maybe they found his rotten bones and never figured out who he was because he never went to a dentist.

Cam asked Paul and Aaron one night if he could bring Wes up to their place, after he got settled back at the farm. Right away they said yes. They said it was important for him to start a regular life again, and if he was anything like Cam, then they were bound to like him. Cam really hopes Wes will still be like Wes, once he's back home. Like the old Wes before it all went wrong. He hopes they're happy. And they never fight, or not too much. And especially never kill anyone.

On the porch now, he's watching the sky. The sun is coming up. There's wisps of bright cloud in the east. Cam sees the big, old solitary elm tree way out there, with its green springtime canopy. If he waits a bit, he'll see the first sunlight hitting the top. Then he'll get in the car.

acknowledgements

The rural Ontario setting of *The Bliss House* is one I know well, even though until recent years I had always been a city dweller.

In the mid-1980s my longtime friend Douglas Chambers acquired a farm property near Walkerton that had been in his family for generations. That landscape, with its yellow brick Victorian farmhouse, became an ongoing and cherished escape from city life for me, my partner Brian, and other dear friends, right up until the terrible day in 2008 when the house was destroyed by a fire. Happily, no one was seriously hurt.

None of the characters or events in *The Bliss House* reflect my real-life experiences in Bruce County. But Douglas, the farm, the community, and the house itself combined to inspire the first words I set down. The rest must have welled up from my subconscious.

I have been blessed with an incredible team of dedicated professionals at Dundurn Press. Special thanks to my wise and sensitive editor, Russell Smith, and to an amazing editorial, marketing, and design team including Erin Pinksen, Rajdeep Singh, and Laura Boyle, for her brilliant cover imagery.

A final thank you to my readers. You are why books are written and are finally the ones whose judgment matters most.